A VERY SIMPLE CRIME

A
VERY
SIMPLE
CRIME

GRANT JERKINS

BERKLEY PRIME CRIME, NEW YORK

Published by the Penguin Group
Penguin Group (USA) Inc.
375 Hudson Street, New York, New York 10014, USA
Penguin Group (Canada), 90 Eglinton Avenue East, Suite 700, Toronto, Ontario M4P 2Y3, Canada
(a division of Pearson Penguin Canada Inc.)
Penguin Books Ltd., 80 Strand, London WC2R 0RL, England
Penguin Group Ireland, 25 St. Stephen's Green, Dublin 2, Ireland (a division of Penguin Books Ltd.)
Penguin Group (Australia), 250 Camberwell Road, Camberwell, Victoria 3124, Australia
(a division of Pearson Australia Group Pty. Ltd.)
Penguin Books India Pvt. Ltd., 11 Community Centre, Panchsheel Park, New Delhi—110 017, India
Penguin Group (NZ), 67 Apollo Drive, Rosedale, North Shore 0632, New Zealand
(a division of Pearson New Zealand Ltd.)
Penguin Books (South Africa) (Pty.) Ltd., 24 Sturdee Avenue, Rosebank, Johannesburg 2196,
South Africa

Penguin Books Ltd., Registered Offices: 80 Strand, London WC2R 0RL, England

This book is an original publication of The Berkley Publishing Group.

This is a work of fiction. Names, characters, places, and incidents either are the product of the author's imagination or are used fictitiously, and any resemblance to actual persons, living or dead, business establishments, events, or locales is entirely coincidental. The publisher does not have any control over and does not assume any responsibility for author or third-party websites or their content.

FIRST EDITION: November 2010

Library of Congress Cataloging-in-Publication Data

Jerkins, Grant.
    A very simple crime / Grant Jerkins. — 1st ed.
        p.   cm.
    ISBN 978-0-425-23830-1
    1. Married people—Fiction.   2. Mentally ill—Fiction.   3. People with mental disabilities—
Fiction.   4. Murder—Investigation—Fiction.   5. Family secrets—Fiction.   I. Title.
    PS3610.E69V47   2010
    813'.6—dc22   2010024877

PRINTED IN THE UNITED STATES OF AMERICA

10   9   8   7   6   5   4   3   2   1

For Andria

ACKNOWLEDGMENTS

Audrey Kelly saw something of value in this story and advocated tirelessly for it, as did Ed Schneider and Brian Overland. Thank you.

I would like to also thank each of the following people who contributed to this book in some significant way: Doug Crandell, Ginger Leonard, Jill Haynes, Bonnie Stacey, Wanda Standridge, Rita Kempley, Tom Kavanagh, Joan Scoccimarro, Ruth Newman, Susan Dyer, Angela M. Olsen, Collin Kelley, and Kate Brady. Terry Curtis Fox suggested the title.

At Berkley Books I want to acknowledge the significant contribution of my editor, Natalee Rosenstein, and my appreciation goes to Michelle Vega for lighting the way.

Literary Agent Robert Guinsler made it look far too easy. Thank you, Robert.

Lastly, I want to state the obvious: that people with developmental disabilities are no more prone to violence

ACKNOWLEDGMENTS

than any other individuals. We are fortunate to live in a
time when institutions such as the one depicted in this
book are closing, and people who were once institution-
alized are now recognized as important contributors to
their communities and workplaces.

PART ONE

I'm crazy for tryin'
and crazy for cryin'
and I'm crazy for lovin' you

—WILLIE NELSON, "CRAZY"

ONE

After our parents' violent and unexpected deaths, my brother, Monty, and I were taken in by our mother's sister and her family. As if to accentuate our already profound sense of displacement, we were delegated to a makeshift bedroom in the basement of our aunt's suburban home, separate from those in the levels above.

As we mourned the sudden and unexpected loss of our parents, the basement seemed an appropriate environment. For us, the basement was not a hardship, though. We shared a dim room in the damp space beneath the house. We grew to love it. We had privacy to experiment with stolen cigarettes and stay up till all hours watching black-and-white crime movies. We were separate from the rest of the family, the strangers above us who shared our blood, and we were rulers, or so it seemed to us, of our own domain.

The basement, being belowground, was completely without light at nighttime. The deepest darkness. One night, I woke needing to use the bathroom and clambered from my bed to make the trip upstairs to the only bathroom in the house. The bathroom was our only connection to the others who lived in the house with us, the need to relieve bodily functions our only acknowledgment to those who lived above. This night, I neglected to turn on the bedside lamp to light my way. Why should I? It was a trip I had made countless times before. I could have easily negotiated the course with my eyes closed. But this time, for whatever reason, somewhere along the way, I got lost.

I think that I became conscious of the darkness. That must have been it. The void of the absolute absence of light. Only a few steps from my bed, I paused along the familiar path. I tried to see my own hand held inches from my eyes, but I couldn't. I was blind. Lost. Frightened.

I began to walk as a caricature of a blind man. Feeling my way. Tapping my foot cautiously in front of me, finding nothing but emptiness. After what seemed hours, I touched the cool, smooth hardness of the painted cement wall. Thinking I had found an anchor, a landmark of familiarity, I relaxed somewhat. I rested for a moment, thinking myself foolish for being frightened earlier, but I soon realized I was still lost. The wall felt alien to me. Porous and somehow obscene. I followed it and followed it and followed it, loathing the foul feel of it, but still it led me nowhere. Panic rose in my throat, tight like a clenched fist. I played my fingers over each painted pore of each cinder block in the wall. It felt as though I had been transported to some crater-blasted alien landscape. A certainty grew in me that soon, my searching hand would touch something cool and wet and elastic. Something alive. I gave in to my fear and forgot my pride. I called out for my brother. "Monty! Monty! Monty!" His bedside light clicked on, and my old familiar world swam into focus. Monty blinked at me and asked what was wrong. I felt like a fool. I was standing alone, in an unlikely corner, like some piece of unused furniture pushed out of the way. I felt shame, but also relief. I stood dumbly caught in the light, my outstretched hand less than an inch from the light switch.

Now I find that I've fallen prey to this unlikely phenomenon once again. I was living my life as I always had, as I believed I always would. I did not stumble blindly toward death; rather, each step of my life seemed preordained, as though it had been planned out a thousand years before I was born. And I took each step with complacent pleasure, knowing I was taking the right path. I strode proudly, if predictably, through my life.

But something went wrong. I faltered. Misstepped.

Somewhere along the way, I got lost.

The courtroom is not what I expected. It is very quiet most of the time. The lawyers murmur their objections when they find something objectionable. They are almost polite in their questioning. Today is the last day of the trial. Today is the day I will be called upon to explain myself, to defend my actions. Monty is my lawyer. Thirty-five years later and I still need my brother to save me from the darkness. He leans over and whispers into my ear, "Today I am my brother's keeper." He stands, handsome as ever, his suit impeccable, his hair receding but still a burnished blond and freshly cut in a boyish style that makes him seem impossibly young, impossibly beautiful. He addresses the judge. "Your Honor, the defense would like to call as its last witness the defendant, Mr. Adam Lee."

I stand. I feel awkward as I push my chair back. The area between the defense table and the witness box seems improbably open and impossibly immense, and the panic of the agoraphobic washes over me. I concentrate on not tripping over my own feet as I make my way into this vast open space. I see the witness seat ahead of me, empty and waiting for my arrival, and I know that it will be years before I can complete the journey to reach it. I glance up and to the left and see the judge watching me. I smile at him stupidly, thinking that he knows what I'm feeling, having seen this drama played out a thousand times before. I feel the twenty-four eyes of the full jury box watching me, gauging me, wondering why I am walking like the hypnotized, the drugged, the undead. Finally, I climb the two steps into the witness box and grasp the chair like an exhausted swimmer touching land.

Looking out into the gallery, I wonder if the reporters will comment on my stilted trek to the stand, my dazed appearance. Then my brother's face fills my vision, and even now, blind from the darkness that surrounds me, I am in awe of his beauty.

"Mr. Lee, after everything that's gone on before this moment, there's really only one question that matters. I'll ask it point-blank. Adam Lee, did you murder your wife?"

Just as Monty has coached me, I do not hesitate with my answer, yet still, in the time it takes me to open my mouth and spit the words out, I can feel the eyes of the jury on me, drinking me, eating me, like the body of Christ.

"No," I say. "No. I loved my wife."

TWO

Rachel had always been a good wife. But at some point, and without my realizing I had done it, I did to her what had been done to me and my brother so long ago. I delegated her to a lower level. She was still there, with me, seemingly an important fixture in my life, as always, but now in a place below me, separate.

Or perhaps it was I who was separate, who had remained separate. Had never left the damp coolness of the lower levels.

She would never leave me; of that I was certain. Her love for me, from the very beginning, was fanatical.

I did not meet Rachel until we were both in our twenties, yet she had never kissed a man, much less the other things. And although her devotion to me was, from the very

9

beginning, that of the born-again convert, I still suspect that had it not been me she found, it would have been another. In the end, her love would have found a blistering focus on any man who could withstand it. It did not have to be me. I could never tell her this, but it is true.

We met at a college graduation party. Her date was drunk and became belligerent when she asked to leave. Already settled into a sober-minded life, I was not drinking and offered her a ride to her dormitory. She accepted. Outside the dorm building, she opened the car door to get out, then hesitated.

"This is silly," she said. "It's graduation night. We should be having fun."

I looked at her, waiting to see what she meant.

"Well, what do you think?"

"I agree," I said, not knowing what I was agreeing to.

She pulled her leg back into the car and closed the door. She leaned across the seat and kissed me on the cheek. "Let's go get some beer."

In her dorm room, we played a drinking game that involved bouncing a quarter off a tabletop and into a glass of beer. We drank the beer and flirted with each other. She told me about her father. How he tried to control her with his money. When she reached to pick up the quarter, I noticed a bubble-gum-colored scar that stretched across her wrist. The scar was raised, textured, and repulsive. She followed my gaze and pulled her arm away.

"That happened a long time ago." She carefully aimed the

quarter. "I used to be a very sad person." She threw the quarter hard against the tabletop. It bounced off the table, arced spinning through the air, and plopped into the glass of beer. I watched the quarter zigzag lazily through the amber liquid until it came to a rest at the bottom of the glass. Bubbles erupted around the quarter and foamed to the top of the glass. "I used to be a very sad person," she repeated, and pushed the glass aside. She leaned across the table. "But now I'm a very drunk person." She kissed me. I hesitated at first. Then I kissed back.

Can I admit it now? Can I acknowledge that on some level, even then, I was attracted to her mental illness? Certainly it was there, like a badge of achievement for all to see. I saw it, stretched and pink-edged across her wrist, and I responded to it. Darkness is drawn to darkness.

THREE

Once, while we were still dating, she caught me appreciating the figure of a salesgirl.

We were shopping in a mall clothing store, and I waited, as all men do, while she tried on different garments. Rachel emerged from the dressing room to get my opinion of the latest choice. I didn't notice her. I was idly watching the salesgirl put away clothes. Rachel gauged the emotion in my eyes and followed my gaze to the stockinged legs of the young woman. A sound escaped Rachel's throat. A sound I had never before heard. It was neither animal nor human. It was inorganic. It was anguish. Rachel seemed to crumple in on herself, as though the horrid sound she emitted were her escaping life essence. I went to her, hands open. She warded me off. "Don't! Don't you! Don't!" Her hands went to her head. Her fingers tore strands, then clumps, of her hair out of her head. Her scalp began to bleed. The salesgirl stared at us, horrified. I have been very careful ever since.

FOUR

"So she's crazy. Guess what? All women are crazy. You know why? Because all men are liars. Like you don't know. You're telling me what? That if this salesgirl says to you, 'Come on in the back, let me suck your dick,' you're gonna say what? No? 'I don't want you to suck my dick even if you are young and beautiful.' Bullshit."

Monty had passed his bar exams the previous year. Whereas I had perfunctorily gone to school and received a degree in business, Monty had soared through his education and was given a junior partnership at a prestigious law firm. It was quite an accomplishment, but then again, Monty usually got what he wanted. What his sunny blond hair and rugged good looks did not bring to him, his sharp mind could figure out a way to obtain. Every year a local magazine listed the city's most eligible bachelors, and Monty's name was invariably at the top of the list. I went to see him at his office. The secretary escorted me in, and I found Monty reclined with his shoes, black leather buffed to a luxurious glow, propped up on his desk, a cigarette clipped between his fingers. Since our father's death, I always consulted Monty with my problems. He was stronger, smarter, and more worldly than me.

"It's not like that," I said.

"It's exactly like that. I know it. You know it. She knows it. Men cannot be trusted. And it drives women crazy."

Monty lit another cigarette, blew a smoke ring. It drifted into my face.

"And she's worth how much? How many millions? She can afford to pull her hair out."

"Please."

"Look, Adam, your track record with women isn't exactly phenomenal. People are starting to wonder, you know."

"This is your idea of advice?"

"I'm just saying that you have a history of running away from girls who want you."

That was a low blow. I was shocked that he would dare mention it at all. He was referring to an incident from our childhood. A girl who vacationed with our family. A girl I had a boyhood crush on. Some extremely unpleasant things happened that summer—including our parents' deaths at the end of it. It was an unfortunate slip on his part.

"You have a history as well," I said. "How many women

has it been now that you've allowed the pleasure of your company?"

"Beyond number." He smiled. It wasn't much of a jab from me. He was quite proud of his reputation as a Lothario.

"Look, so she's a little loony tunes. You say she's pretty. You say she's rich—"

"It's her father's money."

"And he's how old?"

"You're certainly a lawyer."

"Thank you. Want me to be the best man?"

FIVE

Rachel and I married two years later. Was I attracted to her mental aberrations? Does darkness call to darkness?

The product of our marriage was spoiled. Our son, Albert, was born mentally retarded, and as he entered adolescence and physical adulthood, he became prone to unpredictable outbursts of violence. Secretly, I blamed Rachel for our damaged offspring, and she, in turn, secretly blamed me.

We did not know at first that Albert was incomplete. His arrival from the hospital was ripe with hopes and dreams of a secure future. As I suppose happens all too often, we invested the arrival of our son with magical, healing qualities for all aspects of our lives. My job, I believed, would take on new meaning; life would not seem pointless. And Rachel, I'm sure, bargained on reawakened passion from her indifferent

husband and a wider focus to dilute the glare of her maniacal love, saving both husband and son from wilting in the
intense rays of her emotion.

And, indeed, these prophecies seemed to be realized. I
really did find an unremembered vigor in life and a renewed
closeness to Rachel. I felt that our lives were on the right path,
the correct course. And if Albert was a little late in reaching
some of his developmental milestones, surely it was nothing
to worry about. Surely he would soon begin to make up for
lost time and amaze us all with his innate intelligence. But
inevitably, relatives and friends began to voice aloud the
questions that we had not yet dared voice ourselves.

"Shouldn't he be talking by now?"

"He never makes a sound."

"Are all babies this quiet?"

"His eyes. Don't they look strange?"

We took him to many doctors, specialists, organizations,
each with a differing opinion. It was hard to say for sure, they
told us. Difficult to pin down an exact cause. But, in the end,
a diagnosis was agreed upon. No one's fault, they said. Fragile
X. A soft X chromosome. Unavoidable. No way of foretelling.
These things happen.

We resolved, as I imagine all parents in such situations
do, to love Albert. We would raise him, love him as though
he were normal. Rachel carried the brunt of the responsibility. She devoted her life to ensuring the quality of his. She
took him to special classes, hospitals, learning centers. And
through her sheer will, her withering love, she taught him

basic life skills. He learned to perform tasks that the doctors told us he would never accomplish. Dressing himself, feeding himself, bathing, grooming, continence. And when he reached age fourteen, we had the perfect five-year-old. A five-year-old teenager who thought it natural to strike out at those who slighted him in any perceived way. A five-year-old adolescent who put his mother in the hospital for one rigid week after smashing in her skull with a crystal ashtray when she scolded him for a toileting accident.

SIX

I have never cared for my work. It is too clichéd to contemplate, but I took a job with my father-in-law's company, Lawson Systems Financial Risk Management. I arrived every day at eight and spent nine hours behind my desk in my small office. I brought my lunch and ate it at the desk. I signed papers and drew graphs. There was certainly nothing dramatic in my responsibilities. My work was competent, drawing neither praise nor condemnation.

As I say, I have never cared for my work. But during our son's upbringing, I applied myself to the job as never before. And an amazing thing happened. I was successful. Raises followed promotions, and respect followed these. I excelled at the not always legal task of peering into the financial lives of others. At times, my duties were more akin to a hacker than a pencil pusher.

A certain tension remained between me and Rachel, but she enjoyed my success. Rode my coattails. I became, in years, a top executive. Rival companies vied to steal me away. But I remained loyal to my own. I reached a plateau where I could rise no higher. Just as Rachel had reached her own plateau with our son. He was too violent, too unpredictable for her to safely manage. After her injury and hospitalization, a change seemed mandated.

It was at this time that we finally decided to institutionalize Albert.

SEVEN

At first, we visited Albert every week. The halls of the institution were brightly lit and carried sound alarmingly well. It was impossible to discern if the scream you heard was right behind you or yards ahead into the brightness. The smell of industrial disinfectant (a smell I associated with Band-Aids from my boyhood), though it permeated the atmosphere, could not quite mask the odor of human life exerting itself at its most biological level. Rachel's newly permed hair glowed like a curly halo in the bright fluorescent light as we made our way down the corridor. Later, that night, as we performed our dutiful sex act, I would smell vestiges of the disinfectant in the curls.

Albert's suite (Mrs. Jones, the matronly administrator, used this word—*suite*—six times when originally describing to us the accommodations) was nicely, if practically, furnished. No glass, no hard angles, lightbulbs secured behind metal cages, all furniture securely bolted to the floor. On one visit, before entering Albert's room, we stood in the doorway and watched as our son interacted with Jack, his suitemate (another selection from Mrs. Jones's argot).

"Albert, Albert, did you hear what I said to you? I said, good day, sunshine."

Albert, sitting on his bed, uncrossed and then recrossed his legs. He rocked back and forth.

"Albert," Jack said, "did you hear what I said? I called you sunshine!"

Albert continued to rock back and forth, but Jack was insistent. "I called you sunshine! Albert! Albert!"

Albert rocked even faster yet; he grunted and smoothed his hands over his hair. Classic signs of Albert's growing agitation. He yelled at Jack. "Leave Albert alone! Jack, leave Albert alone!"

Jack apparently recognized the danger in Albert's voice. He skulked past me and Rachel, muttering to anyone who might care, "Jeez, all I did was call you sunshine."

Albert saw his parents watching him. He jumped from the bed and ran to us. "Mommy, Daddy! Albert did bad wrong. Albert did bad wrong." *Bad wrong* was Albert's newest catchphrase. He used it whenever he saw us. Apparently, Albert had decided that his sentence at the institution was the result of his wrongdoing. And he was right.

Our visits grew less frequent. Albert aged physically. He

grew into something of a hulk. A mostly silent giant who looked like neither me nor Rachel. At one point, there was talk of a group home for Albert. As Mrs. Jones described it, a group home is a noninstitutional setting for those with developmental disabilities similar to Albert's. A group home is staffed with workers called houseparents. Living in a group home was apparently a great advantage. The list of applicants was long, but Albert was considered a prime candidate. The group home would offer something that Albert would find at no institution no matter how advanced its therapies. It would offer him normalization. Mrs. Jones used this word— *normalization*—in our meetings. Over and over, she repeated the word as though it obtained some magical quality when spoken aloud. *Normalization. Normalization. Normalization. Your son is now normal.*

Or perhaps the magic the word wove was on Rachel and me. *With a wave of the bureaucratic wand, your son no longer lives in a barren institution. You are now free from guilt. Please return to your former lives. Your son now lives in a normal home, just like you. You can visit him there, just as you would visit a son who was normal. You can return to your normal lives. Everything is normal now.*

A month before he was to move to the group home, Albert killed his suitemate, Jack, in a dispute over a pair of socks. We never heard the word *normalization* again. Albert did move, however. He was transferred to a larger facility called the Hendrix Institute, where he is given daily doses of Mellaril, Haldol, and Ativan. The few times we have visited him there, he has been only semiconscious. His clothes were soiled with fecal matter, drool slicked his unshaved chin, and scratches covered his face—self-inflicted from his ragged, broken fingernails. Neither Rachel nor I have ever spoken of objecting to this heavy regimen of antipsychotics and sedatives. Why would we?

EIGHT

After sex, Rachel sleeps. Content. My semen her trophy. Stolen from me and locked secretly away inside. She has me. She will never let me go.

I learned long ago that to deny Rachel her trophy is to risk anything, everything. She will grow suspicious. Become moody. She will smoke incessant cigarettes. Her sleep, if it comes at all, will be broken and restless. I must consent to her rape or suffer the consequences. She will pick fights. Demean my manhood. She will cry, say that I do not love her, never have. Her fingers will seek out her hair, coiling clumps of it. Twirl. Twirl. Twirl. Strands will loosen. Twirl. Bald spots appear. Twirl. Scabs grow. Twirl. I give in. She has won.

After sex I lie awake in the darkness. A victim. I think of Albert. Would things be different if he were here for Rachel to love? As it is, all of Rachel's energies are focused on me. I am Rachel's world. Her work in progress. I wonder if Albert knows the dark. Where is his basement? Where is his dark place? But then I see that he was born to the darkness. He has never lived with the others in the top of the house. The basement, the dark, is all that he knows. He is satisfied, I think.

NINE

In a moment of sudden clarity, I call Monty from my office. When I tell him my plan and what I need from him, he denies me.

"That's fine," I say, not willing to give up this last bit of fortitude I've found. "I'll just hire someone else."

Monty sighs over the phone. "First of all, I'm a criminal defense lawyer. I don't do divorces. Secondly, all I'm saying is give it time. I don't think you're thinking clearly."

Oh, but I am, I am. "You don't understand. She's . . . She . . . When we have sex, it's as if she . . . If she doesn't get it, she gets suspicious."

"Lots of women get a little crazy when they don't get sex."

"No, that's not what—"

"I know, I know. Listen, all I want to know is, is she forty million crazy? That's what her old man's worth. I checked. Are you willing to give up that kind of money? Seriously."

"I don't care about the money."

"You don't? Not the money, not the house, not the car, not the job? Oh, you thought, after you label his daughter as psychotic in divorce court, her father would say, 'No, Adam, your job is safe; as a matter of fact, we're promoting you. Keep the car, too. In fact, keep the house; we'll put the crazy bitch in a loony bin. I'll adopt you. You'll be my heir.'"

But I didn't care, not then, I really didn't. "Are you going to file the divorce papers for me, or do I go to someone else?"

In my mind's eye, I could picture Monty on the other end of the line, grinning one of his famous smiles, all teeth and blindingly white. "Okay, okay. Do this. Wait three months. Three months. Can you do that? If you still feel the same way, I know a guy in family law. One of the best."

I acquiesced, certain that I would feel even more strongly about it in a few months.

But I didn't. The months came and went, and I didn't feel the same sense of urgency. My moment of clarity had passed.

TEN

One night, I work late. I am tracking down the lost funds of James Tritt, an important client. I explore curvy electronic paths in my search for Mr. Tritt's lost money. This is my forte. No human contact is involved, just a faintly glowing computer terminal to light my solitary investigations. I have called Rachel to tell her that I miss her, that I hope to be home soon, but the truth is that I prefer the company of this quietly humming machine to that of my wife. My machine responds to me in ways that I can foresee and easily understand.

My secretary, Grace, has diligently stayed late with me. I imagine, foolishly, that she merely wants to appear ambitious. She drops a stack of folders on my desk.

"How's it coming?"

I blink at her, having momentarily forgotten how to communicate on a purely human level.

"Well, believe it or not, I think I'm finally on to something."

Grace moves around the desk. She stands too close to me, leans over my shoulder to see the computer screen.

"What is it?"

"Well, it seems that Mr. James Tritt isn't always James Tritt."

"I don't get it."

I don't really want to let her into my electronic world, but at the same time I welcome the opportunity to show off my skills. I press a few keys, and confidential bank documents appear on the screen.

"Sometimes he's Jimmy. Tritt named his son after himself, and I think that James Junior has been using his father's identity."

"How can you know that?"

"If I have James Junior's social security number, this program lets me look into his personal accounts at any institution. The deposits and investments correspond to the amounts missing from the father's accounts."

Grace squeezes my shoulder. The gesture is just that—a gesture, a simple nonverbal communication. *You did it. Congratulations.* All the same, I feel awkward. Grace has been my secretary for only a year, and this is the first time that I can recall physical contact between us. The squeeze lingers a moment longer than it should. Then her other hand joins the first. She begins to lightly massage my shoulders. I try to act as though I am grateful, as if I am at ease with this casual contact, while in fact I am not comfortable with it at all. I put my hand over hers. Pat it lightly and pull away.

"Listen, Grace, I'm almost finished here. You should go home."

"You sure? I can stay."

"No, really, you should go."

"You know, I really don't mind staying."

"No."

Later, I call Rachel again. She answers on the seventh ring. Immediately I recognize the alcohol in her voice. I hear the television in the background. She tries to disguise her drunkenness but overcompensates, pronouncing each word with excruciating accuracy. She sounds like a drunk trying not to sound drunk. I know that soon she will dip into her pharmaceutical supply and augment her drunkenness with a carefully chosen pill. Depending on the pill chosen, I know that when I arrive home later I will be greeted by either a catatonic stupor or the ravings of a maniac whose lunacy is directed toward me.

"I'm just wrapping up. Thirty minutes. No more."

I try to sound casual, pretend that I don't know she is drunk. I say a silent prayer for catatonia.

"I love you, too," I say. It is my catechism to ward off evil. The office door opens. Grace stands in the doorway holding a carton of take-out food. I hang up the phone.

"I thought you were going home."

"I figured you hadn't eaten all day. I got Chinese."

After we've eaten, I walk Grace to her car in the underground parking lot. This late at night, the lot is mostly empty. Our footsteps sound lonely. Grace hooks her arm through mine.

"I really appreciate your walking me."

"I really appreciate the dinner."

She tightens her grasp on my arm. "You should come over to my place. Have a drink. Unwind a little."

I don't respond. I try to imagine what it would be like to enjoy the company of a sane woman. I wonder how my life might be different had I chosen another wife. Did I really ever have a choice? Does Grace carry some silent badge of incipient insanity, some telltale sign that she is unstable? Is that why I find myself attracted to her? Or is she what she appears to be—an intelligent, attractive woman? Is this my opportunity for a second chance? I imagine myself making love to this woman, not submitting to her, but enjoying her body as she enjoys mine. I imagine myself gaining strength and insight from her. I imagine this small infidelity changing me in some intrinsic way. I imagine myself leaving Rachel.

"Oh, come on! It would be fun. Live a little."

I feel the change welling up inside me. I feel mischievous, giddy, and alive. "Well, maybe just for—"

A horrible moan oozes from Grace's slack mouth. Her grasp on my arm tightens painfully. Her car is in front of us. The windshield is smashed. The glass is cracked and opaque like a cataract.

"Oh, my God! My car! Jesus Christ. Who . . ."

All four of the tires have been mercilessly slashed. Chunks

and ribbons of black rubber litter the area. A kitchen knife protrudes from one of the tires. I extricate myself from Grace's grip. I have to squat down and leverage myself against the wheel to pull the knife out. I put it in my coat pocket.

"I can't fucking believe this! I can't even fucking imagi—"

I back away from the car. Away from Grace.

"What are you doing?"

I back away. I look at the ground, because I can't look at her. My feet carry me away from her. "I'm sorry. I have to."

"Have to? Have to what? Where the fuck are you going? You can't leave me here!"

"I'm sorry," I say. There is nothing else for me to say.

"You can't leave me here!"

But I can, and I do.

When I get home, all the lights are off. I walk through the dark house and into the kitchen. I take the knife from my pocket and return it to the vacant spot in the cutlery block.

In the bedroom, I submit to Rachel. The sex act is animalistic. She is vicious. She scratches me until I bleed. Scratches herself. She cries out in her climax. Sweaty and blood-smeared, she dismounts me.

Later, we lie facing away from each other. Her breathing is deep and regular. I close my eyes.

"You know that if you ever cheated on me, I'd kill the slut. You know that, don't you? Then I'd kill you."

I know. I know. I know. I know.

"I know."

ELEVEN

After reaching my apogee as a professional, after sentencing my son to the subcellar of psychotropic medications, after surrendering myself to the prison of marriage, I seek out the services of a psychiatrist. I do this by looking in the Yellow Pages of our local telephone directory. This strikes me as pedestrian, but I know of no other way to go about it. I, of course, do not tell Rachel.

My psychiatrist is Dr. Salinger, a gray-haired man with a short-cropped beard. He looks, I think, the way a psychiatrist should look. He strikes me as insightful, intelligent. I tell him that I believe my wife suffers from a personality disorder. I tell him that she is in some way damaged. That she carries a malignant gene. That she passed this rogue gene on to our son. I tell him that I wonder sometimes if they both—my wife and son—might not be better off dead. Rachel out of her misery, free of her tormenting mood swings, and Albert saved from the constant darkness.

Dr. Salinger seems not at all surprised by these unwelcome thoughts that fill my head. Thoughts that, I tell him, reverberate in my skull, picking up speed until they are bouncing back and forth like atoms reaching a critical mass.

"Yes," he says. "I see. I see." I tell him I cannot see. I have been struck blind.

TWELVE

Rachel's father, Benjamin Lawson, my employer, dies suddenly and unexpectedly of a stroke a year later. His entire estate is left to Rachel. We are rich. The death strikes yet another blow to Rachel's fragile world. She deteriorates rapidly. She refuses to leave the house. Any suggestion of venturing outside is met with hostility. Her doctor, who must come to the house to see his patient, prescribes yet another antidepressant, but if the drug has an effect, I cannot see it. Her drinking escalates. Rather than blur her scrutiny of me, the alcohol intensifies it. I am her world.

Years pass and nothing changes. Occasionally I make gestures of fortitude, to gauge if her vehemence has lessened or if my weakness has improved. One day, I find her in Albert's room. The room is still decorated with children's furniture, finger paintings Scotch-taped to the wall. Rachel sits beside the bed in a rocking chair. An overflowing ashtray rests on the bedspread that is bright with cartoon figures. A cigarette smolders between her fingers, a glass of raw scotch nestled between her legs. The rocking of the chair threatens to spill the scotch. She pulls at her hair. Twirls long strands of it. I see small bald spots and crusty scabs in her scalp.

I do not like it when she brings her sickness into Albert's room, mourning for a son who is not dead but may as well be. I open with a mild accusation. "This place smells like a barroom."

"That's because I'm drinking and smoking."

"You're not supposed to drink with Prozac."

Rachel thrusts her hand into her pocket. Pulls out a prescription bottle. She dumps the pale green pills into her drink. She waves the glass at me in a bitter toast and swills the mixture down. She spills most of it. She picks soggy pills off her blouse and inserts them in her mouth. "Fuck it."

"Look what you've become."

"'Look what you've become.' I haven't become. This is what has been done to me. I miss Albert. I want to see him."

"Why don't you go see him, then?"

"Fuck you. I can't, you know I can't."

"How long has it been since you've left this house?"

"I repeat: Fuck you. Bring my boy to me."

"Not with you like this."

Somehow, I've struck a chord. Rachel lowers her head in acquiescence. She sobs. "Go see him. Tell him his mother loves him. Please, Adam, go see him for me."

THIRTEEN

I go to see Albert. Alone. There is some secret, I think, that he is withholding from me. I do not know what it is, only that it is vital.

His room is, appropriately, on the bottom level of the institution. I do not alert the staff to my presence, but go straight to his room. Outside his door, I hesitate. What am I doing here? What are these thoughts of secrets, of solutions? What can this visit bring except pain for me and confusion for Albert? On the door is pasted a piece of poster board with Albert's name finger-painted on it in a deep mauve color. Rachel taught him how to do that, I remember.

From inside the room, I can hear Albert's deep-throated moans. I push the door ever so lightly, and it swings silently inward. Albert lies on his bed, a prone giant. He is naked with the bedcovers pulled down just below his waist. An attendant—not a nurse, but a nurse's helper—stands over his prone body. She is an attractive girl, the attendant. Straight black hair falls over her eyes. I look down and see that her hand moves rhythmically back and forth over Albert's groin. She holds Albert's sex organ in her small, pale hand. It is engorged with blood and angrily red. Just as I allow myself to comprehend what it is she is doing to him, a loud gasp escapes Albert's throat, and then the girl is wiping the viscous fluid from her hand and from Albert's belly with a clean white towel. She looks up at me and smiles. There is no sense of shame in her expression. No sense of having been caught doing something wrong.

"Can I help you?" she asks.

"I'm Albert's father." I can think of nothing else to say.

"Really! Well, it's nice to meet you." She offers her hand to me. "I'm Violet." I stare at her hand. "Oh, I guess I should wash up first." I couldn't believe this was happening. My mind couldn't process the information quick enough. I had just caught this girl molesting my son, yet nothing seemed wrong.

"What were you doing?"

"Oh. Well. It helps him sleep. See?" Indeed, Albert was sleeping soundly. "He doesn't know how to do it himself, and it doesn't seem right that he should have to go his whole life without . . . you know. Does it bother you?"

"No. No, it doesn't bother me."

"Plus, you know how Albert can get agitated sometimes?

Well, this helps him with that, too. A lot of the other attendants are scared to work with him because of what he did."

She was referring to the suitemate Albert had killed.

"How long have you been working with Albert?"

"Not long. I hope you're not mad."

"No, not at all. I understand. I'd like to talk with you about Albert."

"Gee, I don't know if I could today. I'm getting off in a few minutes. Maybe you should talk to the head nurse."

"No. I want to talk with you. The nurses don't even come down here, do they?"

She shook her head.

"You would know more about Albert than any of them would. Let me buy you dinner, and in exchange, you can tell me about Albert, about his life here. A nice dinner."

Violet looked uncertain, then nodded her head.

FOURTEEN

"So it really didn't bother you, what I did?"

"At first, but now I understand. How did you think of something like that?"

"My mother."

"Your mother?"

"Yeah. She told me that when my little brother was a baby, and he would cry for hours, that's what she did to get him to stop."

I had taken her to the nicest restaurant I could afford without using a credit card or writing a check. It was in the same town as the Hendrix Institute, but I didn't worry about being seen with her. My home was in another county.

Violet was impressed with the food and the opulent—to her—atmosphere. After the meal, we talked. At first, our conversation was stilted—we were from different worlds, after all—but we soon picked up a comfortable rhythm.

"That's incredible," I said. "What do you feel when you do it? Is it like any other duty, or do you feel something?"

"I'm not sure what you mean."

All of this, of course, was crazy. I had no business here with this girl. She looked cheap and unintelligent, but all the same, I was drawn to her. And seeing what I had seen had aroused me. It had aroused me deeply. I realized now that I had never been attracted to Rachel. We had sex, and I performed adequately, but I was only playing a role. Doing what I knew was expected of me. Doing, in the end, what I had to do in the institution of my marriage.

"I mean, do you get any satisfaction from it?"

She stared at me for a long time. I was sure she was going to get up, walk out. But she didn't. She drank from her water glass. "Sometimes."

Later, in the car, Violet wrapped her pale fingers around me. I could feel each of the gaudy rings she wore as she moved her hand over me. She cupped her mouth over mine. As I exhaled, she inhaled. We were as a single unit, our air circulating as one. And her hands were not human to me. They were beyond that. Something beautiful and strange working over me. My climax was the most intense I'd ever known. It erupted like a fountain of light. The semen went everywhere, and I thought, *Not this one, Rachel. This is mine. You'll never steal it from me. This time, I win.*

FIFTEEN

In bed that night, I would not give in to Rachel's advances. She cajoled me, but I would not give in. Her sleep that night was fitful. Periods of restless breathing broken by spasmodic jerks of her body. I slept not at all.

The next day, she was laconic, speaking only to complain. I would not go near her, not touch her. When she idly caressed my face, I imperceptibly moved from her. She took out her cigarettes, smoking one after the other.

"Maybe you should slow down. I can hardly breathe in here."

"This is my house. I paid for it."

"Yes, I'm very aware of that."

"I raised our son in this house." This was, of course, her trump card. She played it at every opportunity.

"Well, our son doesn't live here anymore, now does he?"

Rachel ran her fingers through her hair. "You don't love me, do you? You've never loved me, and I've loved you more than I love myself." It was true; she loved me brighter than the sun burned.

"I love you. You know I love you." I simply said it. The same as I had said it thousands of times before. It was a statement, neither true nor untrue.

"You blame me. Don't you? For Albert. Look at me!"

I couldn't look. It was true.

"You hate me. Wish I were dead. I can tell. I'm not crazy."

"I don't think you're crazy."

"Yes you do! I can see it in your eyes. Right now you're afraid I'll do something crazy. You're scared of me."

"Rachel, I'm not scared of you. You're my wife. I love you."

"No you don't. You can't love me. You've never thought of leaving me?"

I remained silent.

"See! See! I knew it! You want to leave!"

"No. You asked me if I'd ever thought about it. Of course I have. All men think about it at one time or another."

"Well, let me tell you, you'll never leave me. Something bad will happen."

She turned from me. Her shoulders were shaking. Then the stringent smell of burning flesh filled the air.

"Rachel! Rachel, what are you doing?" I turned her to me. She held the burning end of her cigarette to the flesh of her forearm. Ground the hot embers into her skin. "See! This is how much I love you! How much do you love me?"

Once again, I gave in. I held her in my arms, took her to our bed. Gave her her trophy.

At that time, I considered myself, too, to be mentally ill, so I never considered censuring Rachel for her psychotic episodes. I never thought of leaving her. How could I? What chaos might ensue? Would she kill herself? Would she acquiesce, bide her time, then hunt me down and murder me? But most of all, I knew that I could never cause her that much pain. No matter how much I had grown to fear her, I could not inflict that kind of pain on her.

SIXTEEN

I met with Violet every week. I think I must have seemed just another patient to her. She took care of me in the same way she took care of my son. We took hotel rooms. Our relationship grew. It grew only because of familiarity. Love was not involved. For her, I was a diversion, a rich man who took her to nice places and gave her what she thought were extravagant gifts. For me, she was an unknown element. A link to my son, yes, and I confess to eroticizing her relationship with my son. She was our secret. A forbidden flower in a secret garden. She was ours together.

For our relationship to seem to Violet to be a normal one, she expected it to grow in traditional ways. She was aware of my wife and accepted the obvious limitations that imposed; in fact, she relished her role of mistress. She had seen the part played out countless times on countless television dramas. She knew what was expected of her and was aware of what she could expect in return. I admired her for this, and reciprocated by playing my role of adulterer to the hilt. In fact, this idea that we were merely actors in a grand and clandestine play appealed to me immensely. To propagate the illusion and to keep her secure in her role, I bought her gifts. As the drama unfolded, the gifts grew more extravagant. I bought her a finely tailored sable coat that hangs in the closet of her ramshackle mobile home and is worth more than five times the value of her trailer. She knew that as a mistress it was her job to make unreasonable demands of my time. It was my part to object but eventually give in. We planned a weekend excursion to the mountains. There was a cabin there that had belonged to my parents and had since passed to me and Monty. We spent several summers of our childhood there, perpetrating what evils boys might perpetrate. This weekend would be no different. I expected to end my relationship with Violet during this weekend. By then, she would have outlived her usefulness.

When I arrive home after an evening with Violet, Monty is waiting for me in the living room. He stubs out his cigarette in the same ornate crystal ashtray that Albert had used to crack his mother's skull.

"Where is Rachel?" I ask, alarmed.

"It's good to see you, too."

"Sorry. Where is she?"

"Upstairs, asleep. She was very upset."

"Not exactly unheard of around here."

"She was upset about this." He tossed a sheaf of legal papers across the coffee table. "And frankly, so am I."

The papers were a guardianship agreement. They named Monty as the legal guardian of Albert should something happen to Rachel or me.

"I would think that you of all people would recognize the necessity of these papers," I said. "If something happens, I don't want Albert to be forgotten in some basement somewhere. Like us."

"You know I understand. You know that. And you should know that you don't need papers for me to look after Albert. I would do it regardless."

"Then I'm failing to see the problem. We seem to be in agreement here. Rachel and I want you to be Albert's godfather, and you've accepted. Let's sign the papers."

"Rachel refuses to sign. And I refuse, too."

"I don't understand. It's for the best. You said yourself—"

"You worry me, Adam. If you had come to me a couple of years ago and wanted to do this, I would have been all for it. Hell, a couple of months ago even, but lately you seem preoccupied. More than that, you don't seem yourself. I worry about you. And now you come to me with this guardianship idea just out of the blue. It's like you're thinking about death. I worry about you."

"Why? What have I done that is so unusual, so bad?"

"You're changing."

"Not for the better, I take it."

"I don't know, you tell me."

"There's nothing to tell."

Monty lit another cigarette and appraised his little brother. We both know that I will always be his little brother, and even where a parent or a spouse can't, the big brother can always spot the lie. And why shouldn't he? He taught the little brother how to lie.

"You're having an affair, aren't you?"

"Are you my brother or my wife?"

"Rachel has already asked me."

"If I'm having an affair?"

"Sure."

"And what did you tell her?"

"That you aren't capable of something like that. That you love her."

"You told the truth."

"Now you tell me the truth. You can't lie to me, you never could. Are you?"

"No."

"You're different, Adam. Something about you. Tell me."

"I do have a secret relationship."

"With who?"

"A psychiatrist."

"A shrink? You? You're the most levelheaded person I know.

"Sometimes I don't feel levelheaded."

"Yeah, well, none of us do all the time."

"I have bad thoughts."

"Me too. Very bad. So what?"

"Unhealthy thoughts."

"Okay, okay. Look, if things are really getting that bad, come to me, I'll help you. You know that I'll always help you. I always have."

Yes, I thought, *like what you did to Denise that summer; that was a big help. What you did to that girl. What you did, you did for me. Helped me to become the man I am today.*

"I always will."

"I know," I said, but it was all a lie. I pushed the papers across to him. "Here, take these. At least think it over some more. I'll talk to Rachel. We'll get it all settled. For Albert's sake."

Many unpleasant things can happen in our childhood, and mine and Monty's was no exception. I do not blame him for the tragedies of my life, and he has in fact saved me from many of these tragedies. I hold no ill will toward my brother. I could never hurt Monty. I love my brother.

SEVENTEEN

That Friday, I make a trip to the institution, but not to see Violet. I go to retrieve Albert.

I had spoken with the doctor at the Hendrix Institute. Laid the groundwork. Albert's behaviors were under control through medication. Thus he was presumably no longer a danger to himself or to anyone else. I plead my case, spoke of the void in my family, Rachel's deteriorating psychiatric condition that now precluded her leaving the house, our need for this. I ended by saying a home visit could afford Albert some sense of connection. I said it could give him a degree of normalization and the doctor's eyes brightened. He consented.

I had Albert in the car with me. He slept his drug-induced

sleep in the backseat. I had his medications in my front pocket and strict instructions from the charge nurse on the administration schedule. "You wouldn't want anything bad to happen if he missed his pills," the nurse had said. Indeed not. Whatever happened, it was going to be dramatic, of that much I was certain. Of late, I had found myself setting up experiences and confrontations to wring the dramatic value from them. I had developed an affinity for it. What with the changes in my life—I'm told drama is about change—I had decided to make each scene count. My fights with Rachel—I suppose that I orchestrated some of them to make her reactions even more histrionic than they normally would have been. Where a single word or gesture might end a fight, I would choose the opposite word or gesture to extend it. To extend the drama. I even relished Monty's concern for my well-being. Where a brief hug or a solemn vow might have put his worries to rest, I chose instead to extend the conflict, heighten the tension.

Rather than walking blindly through my life, I found myself wanting to arrange it in scenes. To make each scene as dramatic as possible. I was becoming a playwright, writing an autobiographical play. And not only was I writing it, I was the star.

With Albert asleep in the backseat, I pull onto our private drive. As I accelerate toward the house, I pass Monty's car. He does not wave or acknowledge me. His sunglasses catch the late-afternoon sun, reflecting the light back at me so that his eyes look like black holes in reverse—pouring out white light rather than sucking it in.

At home, I find Rachel in the kitchen fixing a drink. I kiss her lightly on the cheek, playing my role as I have written it for myself, and myself alone. I see no need for exposition and cut to the chase.

"I'm going away this weekend. Business."

She puts down her drink, turns to stare at me. "What?"

"I have to bail out one of our clients."

"You're not going anywhere."

"I'm afraid I have to. What was Monty doing here?"

"You should know. It was your idea. Here." She handed me the unsigned custody papers. "He wants you to keep these. He says he won't sign."

"Well, we'll just have to find someone who wants to be Albert's godfather."

"No, he loves the idea of being Albert's godfather; it's your state of mind he's worried about."

"My state of mind?"

"He agrees with me that you've been acting strangely."

"Look who's talking."

"Yes, well, abnormal is normal for me, not you. Monty thinks you may be having suicidal thoughts. So do I."

"Only one of us has a history of suicide attempts."

"Yes, dear, that would be me, and, yes, I have the scars to prove it. However, during some of my more lucid moments, I've noticed a change in you."

It is true, I am changing, of course, but I also find it touching that she has chosen to remain lucid for this amateur intervention to save me. I prefer her drugged, with her demons at bay. Nonetheless, I am moved.

"Monty agrees with me. Agrees with crazy old me. He thinks your all of a sudden wanting him to be Albert's godfather is a way of tidying things up before . . . Sometimes people considering suicide put all of their affairs in order before they kill themselves. And, speaking as the only one here who has attempted it, I can tell you that I actually spent three hours finishing a school report before I did this," and she held out her loathsome wrists. "The mind is a funny thing."

"You know, Rachel, the problem with suicide is that everybody talks about it, but no one actually commits it."

"All I'm trying to say is that you're scaring me. You say you have to go away for business, but how do I know that they're not going to find you dead in some hotel room?"

"Because I'm not suicidal. I swear it. Let's make each other a promise. If either of us feels suicidal, we'll tell the other and do it together. No more secrets."

"That's not funny," she says, and the tears begin. She talks through her tears, but I have no trouble understanding her. In fact, it is at times like these that I understand her best. "If you want to fight, great, let's fight. It's the only time you show any emotion anymore. Any passion."

"I don't want to fight," I say, and take her into my arms to comfort her, an action that needed no rehearsal, I've done it so many times before. "It's all right. I'm all right and you're all right. Don't cry. I brought you something. A surprise. He's in the car. Wait here."

I wake Albert. He is sluggish from the medication. I navigate this lumbering giant through the garage and into the kitchen. I hear the bottle of his pills rattling in my pocket. As soon as she sees him, the mad fever leaves Rachel's eyes. "Albert! Oh, sweetie!"

She stubs out her cigarette and rushes to him. She reaches her arms across his massive shoulders. She looks to me and gives me a grateful smile.

Albert grunts and hugs his mother. He speaks in his flat voice. "Albert did bad wrong."

Rachel hugs him even tighter. "No you didn't, sweetie. Mommy loves you. Mommy loves you so much."

I go upstairs to pack my bags.

EIGHTEEN

The mountains are corrupt with fall colors. The trees bleed with beauty. In their colorful prelude to death, the maples turn a violent red. The youngest ones are only now beginning to change into their scarlet death masks. These trees are spotted and mottled with crimson lesions like illustrations in a medical manual. I have little patience for the dainty pastels of the hickory, birch, sycamore, and white oak. My attention is consumed with the maple's garish horror movie colors.

The ride up is mostly silent. I am in a foul mood. Violet makes several attempts at generating conversation. Most of these attempts concern television talk shows and situation comedies and begin with the words, "Did you see . . ." I simply shake my head and stare at the road. In the foothills, we pass a run-down clapboard church. A road sign in front of the church instructs all who pass by to *PREPARE TO MEET GOD.*

By the time we get to the cabin, my mood has lifted. It is as I remembered it from childhood when our family vacationed here, an elegant affair nestled high in the mountains overlooking a small lake. Our first order of business is sex. This is appropriate since it was here that my brother first initiated me into the world of women and what they were to be used for. Afterward, I walk out onto the deck that overlooks Lake Armistead. I stand on the deck, naked and bathed in sunlight. It feels good, I think, the light. I feel at home in the light. I shift my body so that my genitals are thrust forward and fully exposed to the sun, relishing the burn there.

Violet's voice calls to me from inside the cabin. "You're not done yet, are you?"

I walk back inside and Violet draws the curtains behind me. She flops onto the bed and waits for me. "No," I say, "in the light." I jerk the curtains open and sunlight streams over Violet's naked body. I go to her. We nibble and kiss and bite. She climbs atop me, but I push her rudely off. I flip her over. Grasp her hips and pull them upward. Push her head into the pillow and hold it there. Her cries are muffled, and I cannot tell if they are in protest or delight. Nor do I care. I enter her violently, unnaturally.

We hike a portion of the Appalachian Trail. Violet, sore from our encounter yesterday, has great difficulty navigating some of the rockier terrain. In fact, she was still bleeding from my rambunctiousness only this morning. I take a secret pride in this. Pride in my manhood for injuring her so. I catch her looking at me, and the expression on her face is a mixture of respect and fear. I suspect she wonders who I am. Wonders who is this stranger who brutalized her. I don't blame her.

We come to a magnificent waterfall and riverbed with large flat rocks scattered invitingly in the stream. We have not passed any other hikers in over an hour, so I begin to shuck off my clothes. I find myself wanting to be naked all of the time. Violet has to be coaxed, but soon enough she joins me, naked, in the water.

We sun ourselves on a massive flat rock in the middle of the stream. The water rushes coldly by us as we grow dry and warm in the fall sun. I close my eyes and visit my old friend, the dark. Violet rubs her hand lightly over my chest, scratches her nails playfully over my nipples, and asks, "What are you thinking about?" I don't answer. She trails her hand across my stomach, rakes her nails through my pubic hair, tangling it.

"Adam, tell me what you're thinking about."

"About how much I love the sun."

She grasps my penis, manipulates it, awakens it.

"Do you think about your wife?"

This is a scene that she has assuredly read or seen countless times. Get your lover to discuss his wife while you excite him sexually. I am sure the romance racks at bookstands across the country are filled to overflowing with such scenes. No matter, I will let her play it out, as I play out my own.

She gauges the thickness and rigidity of my erection, the barometer of her powers.

"Do you think about Rachel?"

"No, she's in the dark."

She works me with her hands. I see now that this is her power, her way of controlling me just as Rachel controls me. I allow her the control. I think about my brother and the girl I loved a thousand summers ago. And the circle closes.

Her hands move with a speed and grace that seem incompatible. "What else?" she asks me. "What else about Rachel?" She coaxes me just as she coaxes my erect penis to give up its gift.

I blurt out the words just before the semen splashes across my stomach in a stream of white light.

"I think she'd be better off dead."

That night, our last, I rage against Violet. My contempt for her knows no bounds. On the pretext of sexual exploration, she agrees to allow me to live out my fantasies. I tie her wrists and ankles to the four posts of the bed. I use her body for my own selfish ends. My every animal desire is given over to hate and lust. I commit unspeakable acts. I degrade her. In every way the imagination allows, I degrade her.

Afterward, I untie her. Her feet and hands are blue and icy from lack of circulation. She crawls to a cold dirty corner and weeps quietly.

We leave the mountain as we came, in silence. My thoughts are private and not to be shared with the likes of her. There is no longer any need to formally end the relationship. It is over. In her simple mind, I know she wonders. Questions if she is somehow at fault, at fault for my unspeakable behavior. I know that she wonders if this is not what she deserves. On some collective level, she feels that she somehow deserves such treatment. I know these things, because my brother taught me well. I can already feel Violet pulling away; my actions overrode even the hardiest of abuse syndromes. I know she will never contact me again. I made sure of that last night.

A billboard looms ahead. *SEE LINVILLE CAVERNS.* It calls to me, a cheap roadside attraction, but I know I must see it. Its dark recesses will present me with an opportunity to test my newfound self.

We pull into the dusty lot. Violet refuses to get out of the car, but I insist; I will continue to have this power over her until I allow her to let herself be free of me. I must go in, but I can't go in alone. My transformation is not yet complete enough for that. I still need a comforting hand in the dark places. And once I no longer need even that, I will need nothing. More important, I will need nobody. A tacit agreement passes between us. She will go in, but this is the last experience we will ever share together.

I spot a line of tourists waiting outside the massive oak doors that have been built into the side of Linville Mountain. We get in line behind a gray-haired couple wearing matching red satin jackets emblazoned with the head of a toothy bulldog. The man, his hair clipped in a military-fashion flattop, puffs on a briarwood pipe. The pungently sweet tobacco smoke wafts from his mouth and wisps about on the breeze. The woman, gray with a face of folksy friendliness, turns to us, smiles, and turns back around. She turns again and gives Violet an appraising look.

"Honey, didn't you bring a sweater or such? It's dark and damp in there. They say it stays fifty-two degrees in there year round."

Violet shakes her head. "No, I didn't know. I didn't bring anything."

The woman turns to her husband. "Herbert, give her your jacket. She looks cold." Herbert shrugs off his jacket, the red satin iridescent in the autumn sun.

Violet shakes her head. "No, really, please, I . . ."

I think I know what Violet is feeling. Dirty and ashamed. She does not want to sully this man's jacket with her shame-ridden body.

"Yes, you can, and you certainly will," Mrs. Herbert insists.

Herbert himself jumps in with, "I'd rather a beautiful young woman such as yourself wore it than an old man like me. Besides, I'm hot-blooded, right, honey?" He pats his wife's behind, and Mrs. Herbert rolls her eyes comically.

Violet cringes away from the proffered jacket. I take it from Herbert's hand and drape it across Violet's shoulders, knowing that the weight of the garment of this good man sickens her. Smiling at Herbert, I offer my left hand for him to shake. It is an old trick my likewise left-handed brother taught me. A left-handed person must make certain conces-sions to the right-handed world, but when instigating a handshake, if you offer the other party your left hand, it confuses them and gives you a subtle psychological edge. Herbert does not disappoint me. He stares nonplussed at my hand, feeling, as I know, foolish and awkward. Finally, he grasps my hand in both of his. I have, through the ritual of the male handshake, reduced his role to that of an old blind woman.

"Thank you, Herbert, Mrs. Herbert," I say.

Mrs. Herbert beams at me. "You two make such a nice couple. Are you married?"

I now hate her as much as I hate him. Her smile is crooked and her teeth stained. They are everything I will never be. They are everything that was stolen from me. They are commonplace and ordinary. They are normalcy. Already nervous about entering the cave, I find that I want to hurt this old woman. I want to make her feel bad.

"My wife recently passed away," I say, reveling in it. "Violet's been a good friend to me."

"Oh, I'm so sorry to hear that."

"Don't be. She was a real bitch."

Mrs. Herbert's face immediately loses its former openness. The folksy friendliness is gone. The Herberts turn away from us and no longer acknowledge our presence. They will not have the nerve to ask for the jacket back after the tour.

In the cavern, it is indeed dark and damp. Our group files in under scattered strings of electric lights that struggle vainly to push back the darkness. We make our way down into the cavern, and, indeed, it is very cold. Water trickles down the limestone walls. It drips from the strung-out lightbulbs. Multicolored stalactites and stalagmites hang and grow every-where. Impressive rock shelves fan out in intricately curved shapes. And everywhere, lurking in every corner, is the dark-ness. We pass through magnificent archways of colorful, wet stone. Our tour guide, a pale teenage girl given to snapping her gum, leads us deeper and deeper into the cavern. She is informative if not somewhat bored by nature.

"The caverns were first discovered in 1822 and were later used by deserters of both the Union and Confederate armies. On the rock shelf to your left, you can see the remains of a campfire the deserters built to ward off the constant cold and dark."

We all turn to look. The combined breath of our group hovers above us in a ghostly condensation.

"If you'll walk over here, you can see our underground stream. The trout that swim in this water are unlike any other freshwater fish on earth."

She shines her flashlight into the stream.

"They're blind. Thousands of generations of living with-out light has caused them to no longer rely on eyesight to hunt."

I peer over into the stream. A fine sweat, despite the cold, has formed on my forehead and under my arms. The fish I see are cumbersome and preternaturally pale. Bulbous, opaque tumors grow in the place of eyes.

"Right now we are standing under a mile of solid rock. This cavern exists in total darkness—a darkness so pure, they say a human being would go blind if subjected to it for any length of time."

I look uncertainly at the surrounding rock walls. They seem to be crouching imperceptibly inward, wanting to consume me with their dark secrets. The tour guide reaches out and places her hand on a toggle switch bolted into the rock. Heavy-gauge electrical wiring runs to the switch. Inwardly, I flinch.

"Okay, this is the part of the tour where we turn off the lights. If anybody has any small children who are afraid of the dark, or for whatever reason, we can skip this part. Anybody?"

Her words chill me. They echo my wedding ceremony to Rachel. *Should anyone here have cause why this man and woman should not be married, speak now or forever hold your peace.* But no one spoke up. I was given to the dark. *Oh, please, please let some small child cry out in fear. Don't let them plunge me into the darkness. I've only just escaped the dark. Don't let it take me again. I may not come back.*

"Okay. Ladies and gentlemen, you are about to experience something few humans ever experience in their lifetimes."

Sweat trickles from my armpits and slides icily down my sides. I reach out for Violet's hand, but she pulls away from me. I am alone.

"You are going to experience absolute darkness. The total absence of light."

The tour guide throws the light switch, plunges the cavern into blackness. And I am transported. I am the boy once again. The boy stumbling in the dark who grew into the man stumbling in the dark. The lost boy who grew into the lost man. And I wait and I pray. I pray, yes, but for whom? Who else? Who have I always prayed for? Prayed to? I pray to Monty. I pray for Monty to save me yet again. To set me free of the dark. But I am free. I set myself free. Yes, I set myself free. I know this. I cannot be here again. I cannot. I will not. I will not. I am free.

The lights come on. And yes, it is true. I am free.

NINETEEN

I put my key in the lock. It clicks along the familiar path and opens the door. The sun is setting behind me. I walk through the front door of my house.

Albert sits in a corner, alone. He rocks methodically back and forth. He chants to himself.

"Albert did bad wrong. Albert did bad wrong. Albert did bad wrong."

The smell affronts my nostrils. I know immediately what it is. Excrement and urine, dried and days old, but also something underneath these smells. The smell of death.

Rachel's body lies prone on the living room carpet. The ornate crystal ashtray lies beside her. A bit of her scalp, the hairs still attached, is stuck in a crevice of the crystal. The gash in her head is unthinkably deep and profane, like a flower trying to bloom. But bloom it shall not. The blood, coagulated in the carpet beneath her head, has dried into a blackened crust. Lethargic autumn flies buzz around her open eyes.

I can think of nothing else to do. I call Monty. He tells me to remain calm. But I am calm, I tell him. He tells me to hang up the phone and call an ambulance and then the police, and then to call him back. I do. When I call Monty back, he tells me he knows a man in the prosecutor's office. He will help me. I thank him and hang up.

I look over at Albert. He continues to rock and chant. And I know, the play has begun. I look over to Rachel. Her body has already started to bloat. And yes, it is true. The play has begun.

PART TWO

That's all it takes, one drop of fear, to curdle love into hate.

—JAMES M. CAIN,
DOUBLE INDEMNITY

TWENTY

Leo Hewitt sat behind his small desk in his small cubicle in the very large criminal courts building, his mostly bald head bent over a furniture catalog. The rest of the cubicles, a small warren of them, were deserted now, the other workers having left hours ago. A small lamp cast a dim light on the catalog spread out before him. He turned the page and smiled wistfully at a photo of an impracticably huge and impracticably priced mahogany executive's desk. He rubbed a stubby finger respectfully over the photo in an attempt to feel the grain of what looked to be deeply stained, highly polished wood. He felt only paper. Beside him, a cigar, stubby and thick like his fingers, smoldered in a cracked glass ashtray. He kept the ashtray hidden in his desk for times like these when he was alone in the office. He reached for the cigar, but his hand passed over it and grabbed instead a felt-tip pen. He uncapped the pen and circled the photo of the mahogany desk. He also circled a photograph of an elegant leather desk chair on the opposite page. The pen jerked and made an imperfect circle when the phone squawked at him in an inelegant electronic simile of a bell. He answered the phone before the first ring was over. His gaze never left the catalog.

"Leo Hewitt. Mr. Lee, how are you? Okay, Monty. How are you, Monty? Oh, I'm sorry to . . . Okay. Uh-huh. Uh-huh. No, no problem. That's not a . . . Sure."

Leo switched the phone to his other ear. He pushed the catalog aside and picked absently at a piece of laminate peeling away from the surface of the pressboard desk.

"Peachtree Battle, yeah, I know where that's at. It would be my pleasure. I'm happy to help out. Especially at . . . Really. Anytime. That's what I'm here for. Okay."

Leo hung up the phone. He scratched his head and was again surprised at its smoothness. He was only thirty-nine and had lost the majority of his hair to male-pattern baldness in a span of just under six months. It had fallen out so quickly that he'd gone to see a doctor, scared it was a symptom of some underlying medical problem. Something malignant. It wasn't. The doctor had told him to try Rogaine if he was concerned about his physical appearance. Leo went to the drugstore and priced Rogaine. He could afford to go bald, but he couldn't afford to grow the hair back. And now when he looked in the mirror, a stranger, an old-looking stranger, looked back at him.

He was only thirty-nine in a philosophical sense. But in a professional, business sense, he had been thirty-nine for quite some time. He was thirty-nine years old and had done damn little with his life. The junior deputy prosecutor of the district attorney's office. They'd made the fucking title up just for him. Didn't know what else to do with him, he supposed. Oh well, he was happy to have a job. Happy to be everyone's errand boy. Happy to be the simpleton who had fucked up, but hey, let's keep him around the office for old times' sake, what the fuck. Happy to say "How high?" when Monty Lee, the biggest ambulance chaser in Atlanta, told him to jump. *Yes, Mr. Lee, No, Mr. Lee. Could I lick your sphincter for you, Mr. Lee?* Yes, he was damn happy to be Leo Hewitt. *Call you Monty? Why yes, Mr. Lee, of course, Mr. Lee. Your brother's wife has been murdered? Why, Mr. Lee, what on earth are we gonna do? Lawsy, lawsy me. No, no, no, no, you stay home cozy and snug. I'll be happy to drive out there. What are friends for, Mr. Lee?*

And what truly sucked was that he really was going to drive out there. On the possibility that the favor might be remembered. On the possibility that Monty Lee might think of him when an associate's position opened at Lee's law firm. On the chance that he might be able to start fresh, to make a new name for himself, to get out of here, to get out of this fucking cubicle.

Leo picked up his cigar from the cracked ashtray and

puffed it back to life. He thumbed through the catalog one last time, retrieved the felt-tip pen and circled a picture of an ornate crystal ashtray. Lalique. $479.00.

He closed the catalog and hid it, and the ashtray, away in his desk.

Leo liked to cruise the more exclusive Atlanta neighborhoods on his days off, and as always, when he turned onto Peachtree Battle Road, he was in awe of the houses. They quietly screamed money, and not just money, but old money. The land the houses sat on would by itself be worth over a million for each lot. Leo lived in a one-room flat off Ponce de Leon Avenue with the prostitutes, drug addicts, and male hustlers. He craned his head to look around at the old houses bought with old money; nope, no crack whores in this neighborhood.

The house was easy to find. Two police cruisers and an ambulance were parked in front, their lights throbbing red and blue in the quiet October night. Leo parked his rust-flecked Nissan pickup truck behind Adam Lee's shiny black BMW.

The coroner, Travis Vedder, looked on as two attendants loaded a white PEVA body bag into the back of the ambulance. As it was loaded onto the meat wagon, Vedder patted the shape under the heavy-gauge plastic material. A patrolman handed Vedder a clipboard. Vedder spat a healthy stream of tobacco juice into a foam cup that was nestled into his shirt pocket, then took the clipboard from the patrolman and signed off on it. Leo walked up behind Vedder and slapped him on the back. "Travis! All your staff call in sick?"

"Monty Lee called. Asked me to see to this one personally."

"Same here."

Vedder cocked an eyebrow over his steel-rimmed glasses. The blue and red flashing lights were reflected in the round lenses and Leo couldn't see the man's eyes, only the lone eyebrow that was arched disdainfully over them. Vedder grunted unintelligibly and spat another rivulet of brown juice into his foam cup.

"Hey, you ever hear of mouth cancer?"

Vedder spat again. This time on Leo's shoes.

"Okay, okay. You made your point."

Leo took out one of his fat cigars and bit off the tip.

He spat it on the coroner's shoe. He began to search his pockets for a light, but when he looked up, Vedder was holding out a match that flared up in Leo's face.

From inside the house, Adam Lee watched the short bald man accept the light the coroner offered him. He watched as the coroner slid his wife's body out of the back of the ambulance. He watched as the coroner unzipped the bag and pointed out something to the man with the cigar. The man with the cigar took two steps backward, away from the body. Then the coroner pointed to the house and back to the body. The man with the cigar nodded his head and set off for the house.

* * *

"Mr. Lee?"

"Yes?"

"Oh, wait a second."

Leo ducked back out the door and ditched his cigar in a bed of azalea bushes.

"Sorry 'bout that. Leo Hewitt."

Adam stood and offered his hand to Leo. Leo began to reach out to shake, but realized that something was wrong. He hesitated a moment, retracted his hand, then offered his left hand instead.

"You're a southpaw?"

"Yes, sometimes I forget."

"Not a problem. Anyway, I'm the assistant deputy prosecutor with the DA's office. Fulton County. Your brother called me. Said to tell you he was sorry he couldn't be here. Asked me to take care of you."

Leo took a look around the house. Old money or new, it was damn impressive. His eyes took in a Queen Anne dining room set to the left, a monstrously opulent Tiffany dragonfly lamp scuttled to one corner of the living room, a teakwood breakfront, original abstract paintings on the walls, all the creature comforts. On the black leather couch, looking out of place, sat Albert Lee. Drool slicked his heavy chin.

"Is this Albert?"

Adam nodded and watched as Leo squatted down in front of his adult son.

"How ya doin', Albert?"

"Albert did bad wrong."

"What happened? What did you do?"

"Albert did bad wrong."

Leo stood up and turned to Adam.

"Does he understand?"

"No, not really. He's hurt her before. Never anything like . . . I mean . . . I just don't know what to say. How to react."

"You're in shock. It's understandable. I can't say how sorry I am. For your loss."

Adam stared at the floor. His eyes were drawn to the dark stain hardening in the carpet. He spoke to the stain, not to Leo. "Thank you."

"We'll need to get Albert somewhere where he can be safe and accounted for."

"Of course."

Leo looked at Adam, waiting for the man to look up, but he didn't.

"Is there anything else, Mr. Lee?"

Adam stared at the floor and shook his head. "No, no."

"Are you sure?"

Adam didn't respond.

"I understand you were away when . . . the incident occurred."

"Yes, I went away for the weekend."

Leo rubbed his hand lightly over his bald head, again surprised at its smoothness.

"With a friend?"

Adam finally looked up, stared into Leo's eyes, and suddenly Leo could feel the syndrome and everything changed. The syndrome where they try to tell you with their eyes. Where they try to get their eyes to convey what their mouths will not. But what could this guy need to get off his chest?

"Yes. With a friend."

And it hit him. A cheater. The guy was a cheater. And now the poor schmuck thought this was his punishment for cheating on his wife.

"Maybe you should tell me her name."

And the eyes told him he was right. The eyes said *Thank you* even as the mouth turned defensive.

"Violet Perkins. Does it matter?"

"Probably not. Here, I don't have any cards, but let me give you my number." He scribbled on a scrap of paper and handed it to Adam. "Look, why don't you have Ms. Perkins call me. She can confirm your story and we can put it to rest, just between us."

"I would appreciate that. I loved my wife."

Maybe you did, but your eyes didn't love her.

"I know. I know you did, Mr. Lee."

TWENTY-ONE

The coolness was the first thing that hit him when Leo walked into the basement of the coroner's office. That and the death smell. A lump rose in his throat even before the smell registered. He knew it was just his imagination, but Leo believed that he could actually taste the decay in the air. He walked through several swinging doors deeper and deeper into the morgue, until he found Vedder in the last autopsy room. Vedder stood hunched over the body of an elderly man. Leo couldn't help but notice that the cadaver suffered from the same male-pattern baldness as he did, only the top of the cadaver's bald skull was separated from the rest of him. He watched as Vedder pulled a dripping organ from the gaping hole in the cadaver's chest and plopped it into the grooved scale that hung over the examining table. Leo felt the lump in his throat move up an inch or two. The scale always bothered him. It reminded him of the one in the butcher shop his mother used to drag him to when she did her Saturday shopping. In the butcher's case, Leo would stare horrified at the tripe and cow's tongue offered for sale. Occasionally, the butcher would have pig brains for sale behind the cold glass. And speaking of brains, it looked like that was what was going on Vedder's scale next. Leo had to massage his throat to keep the gorge down.

"Hey, Travis, anything unusual on the Lee woman?"

Vedder put down his scalpel and picked up a foam cup with his bloody, gloved hand. He peeked out at Leo over the rims of his glasses and spat into the cup.

"Unusual? No."

"What were your findings."

"You can't read?"

"Yes, despite the rumors, I can read. But I like hearing it from your smiling face."

"It must really suck."

"How's that, Travis?"

"To have been the big man. And now you're the little man. They won't even let you read the autopsy reports. That must really suck."

"Yeah, you know what, Travis? It does suck. It sucks like you wouldn't believe. Thanks for reminding me. Oh, and by the way, fuck you."

Leo turned to leave, his nausea momentarily eclipsed by his anger.

"Wait."

Leo turned back to Vedder and followed the stoop-shouldered man to a wall of cadaver drawers. Vedder pulled out one of the drawers and unzipped the plastic body bag that held Rachel Lee's corpse.

"So whadda ya wanna know?"

Leo looked down at the body. He could feel the coldness radiating off it. The absence of life.

"I want to know what happened."

"She got hit on the head."

"No kidding. I thought maybe she had a heart attack."

Vedder spit into his cup and wiped a spidery thread of tobacco juice from his chin. Leo thought, *I wonder if it'll fuck up my image if I faint?*

"Nope, impact to skull resulting in depressed fracture. Traumatic subarachnoid hemorrhage."

Vedder pulled a huge magnifying glass from his pocket and positioned it over the wound in Rachel Lee's head.

"See this?"

Leo worked to steady his voice. "Yeah. It's a great big gash in her head. So?"

"Look closer. Around the edges of the wound."

Leo, very much against his better judgment, leaned in closer, and then, under the magnifying glass, he thought he could see faint threads of what could only be tiny shards of glass. "It's glass. So?"

"Not glass, crystal. Very expensive crystal."

"The kid hit her with a crystal ashtray. I know that already."

"How am I supposed to know what you know and what you don't know?"

"Well, what else can you tell me? Is there anything unusual? Anything out of the ordinary?"

"Generally speaking, I would say that being killed by a crystal ashtray is out of the ordinary."

"Well, surely to God there's more you can tell me than that."

"Actually, there is. Stand back a little. Look at the wound as a whole."

Leo did just that, but all he got for his efforts was a little sicker to his stomach. "What?"

"The angle, the degree, the location. What does it tell you?"

"That she got hit hard."

"That whoever hit her, hit her from behind, was taller than she was, and was probably left-handed."

"That's not exactly a bloody glove."

Vedder shrugged and spit into his cup. "If it doesn't fit, you must acquit."

TWENTY-TWO

Leo stood outside the door for a minute. The lettering on the door read *PAULA MANNING, ASSISTANT DISTRICT ATTORNEY.* Three years ago, he remembered, it had been his name on the door. Three years ago Paula Manning had been a deputy prosecutor working under Leo Hewitt's supervision. Three years ago things had been a lot different. Three years ago he had been the assistant district attorney and a likely candidate for becoming the youngest district attorney in the county's history. But that was three years ago. That was before the Guaraldi case.

Leo knocked on the door.

"Open!"

He stuck his head into the office and saw Paula Manning

reclining in her desk chair, her stockinged feet kicked up on her desk, a hamburger and fries resting in her lap.

"Hey, got a minute?"

"Leo, my loyal and trusty servant, come in."

Just as he was often shocked at his own sudden hair loss, Leo found himself taken aback at the changes the last few years had wrought on Paula. She had once been very pretty, and he supposed she still was, but now Paula's features had an angular sharpness to them that hadn't been there even a year ago. She was the same old Paula, maybe fifteen pounds lighter and with lines setting in around her tight mouth and open brown eyes. The weight loss and stress lines had given her a hardness that had never been there before. At least on the surface.

"So, Paula, how they hangin'?"

Paula pretended to adjust her crotch. "A little to the left, actually. What can I do for you, Leo?"

"Well, actually, I was wondering what the status is on that Lee thing."

"Lee . . . Lee . . . Lee. Oh, yeah, the retard did it. Did the same thing five years ago. The family doesn't want formal charges, neither do we. Right now he's on the locked floor at the Hendrix Institute pending a judge's order for placement at the state forensic facility. Maximum security. Seems pretty cut-and-dried."

"Yeah, it seems pretty cut-and-dried, but according to the coroner's report—"

"The coroner's report? Since when do you have access to my files?"

"I don't. I just talked to the guy. I mean, I was there that night, so I'm interested. That's all."

"Yeah, well you know, I still don't know what the hell you thought you were doing by going out there. Your job is to prosecute delinquent traffic violations. If Bob found out—"

"How would Bob find out? Are you gonna tell him? What? You think I enjoy hanging out in traffic court? I mean, goddamn it, Paula, gimme a break. You used to work for me. How do you think that makes me feel?"

"Well, now you work for me. I would think that you'd be used to it by now. What do you expect from me? Should I resign because your feelings are hurt?" He was making her feel uncomfortable. Didn't the fucker know who got him his lousy job in traffic court? She was sure it was humiliating, but, goddamn it, it also paid the bills. And wasn't that what he wanted when he came to her begging for a job? And she had wanted to help out. She felt sorry for him and had gone to Bob to see what he would let her throw his way. And really, she and Bob had shared the same concern about the situation. It wasn't that they held a grudge, it was that something like this might happen. That Leo might start bringing up the past. He might try to remind her of the way things used to be. He might make her feel uncomfortable.

Paula took a bite from her burger and asked, "What is it you want from me?"

"Just a chance. To do something besides speeding tickets."

"Ever since what happened, you've been looking for that big break. A way to prove yourself again. I know that. I respect that. But, Leo, you might as well face it, no one's ever gonna forget what happened." She felt bad. That was a low blow, but Christ, he was asking for it. What did he expect from her?

Leo nodded his head. "Yeah, I know. No one's ever gonna forget. Least of all you." He turned to leave. And the shrug of defeat that passed through his shoulders was too much for her. She wasn't fucking heartless, was she? She had, after all, once worked for this man. This pathetic excuse for a man who made her decidedly uncomfortable. She wasn't a shrew, after all. For God's sake, the man only wanted to feel like a man again. Who would it hurt if he asked a few questions?

"Hold on."

"What?"

"So what did he say?"

"Who?"

"The coroner. Vedder. What did he say?"

"He, uh, he said the wound, the wound was caused by a blow to the head with a blunt instrument inflicted by a left-handed individual."

"So?"

"So the kid's right-handed. I called the hospital."

"So?"

"So he's retarded, not ambidextrous."

"Ambi-what?"

"Ask me about the husband."

"What about the husband?"

"He's a lefty."

"So are about fifty million other people—including me. Do you think I killed her?"

"I don't know, did you?"

"Leo, you are a kind and faithful servant. Some day you're gonna make it big. Maybe even sit here again. In the big chair. I feel it. I really do. What's your point?"

"If nothing else, what was the son doing home alone with the mother? Feels a little bit like a setup. I wanna talk to the husband some more."

Paula picked up a French fry. Swabbed it in a pool of ketchup. "So, who's stopping you?"

TWENTY-THREE

It had been three years since his fall from grace, but it had been two years before that when Leo had first heard the name Frank Guaraldi.

Prosecuting bad guys was all he'd ever wanted to do. When he was a boy, countless television programs had instilled in him the ideal of fighting for justice as a worthy pursuit, but it wasn't until after his mother had been taken in by a scam artist that he knew for sure he wanted to be a prosecutor. A man had come by the house one day shortly after Leo's father had been taken out by a massive heart attack while cutting the lawn. The man who came to the door that day had been smartly dressed and neatly groomed. He introduced himself as Samuel Abdul, investment counselor. Mr. Abdul had ended up talking Mrs. Hewitt into investing her dead husband's insurance money in an overseas petroleum company. Mr. Abdul had shown her conclusively, using charts and projected fuel prices, that she could easily triple her money, or more. Dorothy Hewitt had vivid memories of the 1970s oil crisis. She could remember a time when the idea of gasoline selling for as much as a dollar a gallon was laughable. But it had happened. And then some. But what had ultimately swayed Leo's usually levelheaded mother was Samuel Abdul's insistence that this was her golden opportunity to secure for her son's future, for his education. She had signed over the entire insurance premium and was given a piece of paper entitling her to a thousand shares of an oil company that had never existed. Abdul, who apparently couldn't leave well enough alone, kept pulling the same scam all over town, always targeting recent widows. Once he was caught, Leo's mother had promptly filed charges along with eighteen other people the man had cheated. Using the money he had scammed from his mostly poor victims (who besides the poor would believe in such easy money?), Abdul had hired the best lawyer dirty money could buy. It was at this time that Leo, only twelve and wanting revenge for his mother, had decided that he wanted to be a prosecutor. To defend the defenseless. The prosecutor who handled the case had been a dedicated, intelligent, resourceful man who systematically dismantled every defense strategy the scam artist's well-paid lawyer tried to mount. Leo sat with his mother in the courtroom every day of the trial, completely entranced with the legal battle that was waged there on his mother's behalf. Even after the trial, Leo would sometimes skip school and spend his days in the county courthouse watching small legal dramas played out. Abdul's trial lasted less than a week, and although others might have given up or simply gone through the motions, this public prosecutor had persevered and ultimately won back his mother's money and sent Samuel Abdul to jail for eight years. The prosecutor had even helped Mrs. Hewitt figure out a more conservative way to invest her inheritance, and seven months before she died, Leo's mother saw him graduate cum laude from law school.

As a deputy prosecutor Leo had been assigned to the team handling the Guaraldi case, although, at that time, no one had yet heard the name Frank Guaraldi. The case was simply known as the torso murders. It was already one of the longest and costliest unsolved cases in the county's history. Certainly it was the highest-profile case any of them had ever been involved with, and a legitimate suspect had not even been named yet. Leo's work on the case eventually earned him the position of prosecutor, then lead prosecutor, and, once Guaraldi had been fingered as the most likely suspect, Bob Fox had appointed Leo to the post of assistant district attorney. It was rumored that if he could bring the Guaraldi matter to a successful conclusion, he was an odds-on favorite to go on to become the youngest district attorney to ever hold the seat.

The whole thing started with an arm. A severed arm found in a drainage ditch on a rural road outside Atlanta. The arm had been eaten at by animals and was badly decayed but obviously that of a child. Decomposition had robbed the forensics team of any hope of a print ID. Only one clue offered any chance for identification. A toy ring had been found on the middle finger of the severed arm. It was a cheap plastic thing that only a child would wear. The type of toy that could only be bought out of a bubble gum machine, with cheap gold lamination that was chipping away from the pale plastic base. Investigators tracked down the Chinese manufacturer of the ring, and then the importer, and from there the distributor. The distributor's records listed several vendors in the Atlanta area. The ring went in a seventy-five-cent machine of which there was one vendor who maintained only one such machine. That machine was located in an arcade in the Little Five Points area of downtown Atlanta. This was a definite starting point, the first real lead they had had to follow up on. All missing-persons reports from the city police department were culled for the previous two years, and from those reports investigators pulled the names of children between ages four and twelve, and from this list was pulled only those missing children who had lived within a twenty-mile radius of the Little Five Points neighborhood. A group of officers was dispatched to interview family members of the missing children.

The temperature had peaked at a record-breaking one hundred one degrees that July day, and Officer Lyle Davis was thinking only of a cold beer when he knocked on the door of the last address on his list. Donny Easton, missing for three months. He showed the photo of the plastic gold ring to Mrs. Easton, a huge and solidly built woman. Her eyes widened and hope bloomed on her face. Donny had worn one just like it. Never took it off. Officer Davis explained the circumstances of the ring's discovery and watched Mrs. Easton crumple to the floor. He'd forgotten all about the dreamed upon beer. More body parts were found. Arms, legs, sometimes just a finger, twice an ear, and one time a severed head. Always children. Never an entire body. Some of the body parts led to identification, but many did not. Each time a piece was found, the national media descended on the city like vultures following the scent of carrion. The police department, and in particular the mayor, were singled out for criticism for allowing the slaughter of children to continue. Gestures such as a hotline number for tips and a dusk-till-dawn curfew were made to appease the frightened population, but no real progress was made.

The death count stood at nine. Possibly nine, because not a single complete body had thus far been recovered. The city lived in fear; parents existed in a constant state of maniacal paranoia. Neighbors reported neighbors for eccentric behavior. An anonymous caller to the tip line gave the name of a man, James Nice, a bachelor with no children, who was seen purchasing dolls and hacksaw blades in a local K-Mart. Nice was investigated and found to be blameless (the blades were to cut a section of burst water pipe in his garage, the dolls for his niece's birthday), but his name was leaked to the media. They called him a person of interest. News crews set up mobile studios outside his house. His face was seen on television and in newspaper photos with captions that capitalized on his ironic name. Within a week of the tip line call, the chief of police declared him no longer a suspect, and the media pulled away. By then, Nice, a recovering alcoholic, had turned to bouts of heavy drinking and antisocial behavior. He yelled at strangers in the street and took to shoplifting. He lost his job. Lost his house. Three months after being cleared as a suspect, he was found dead in a homeless shelter lying facedown in a pool of his own vomit. Nice's family sued the city and were eventually awarded four point seven million dollars.

Frank Guaraldi. He and his wife, Janice, ran the Little Wonders day care and after-school center in College Park. When the ninth victim of the Torso Killer was identified as Gwendolyn Peters, Leo Hewitt, as the district attorney's liaison to the police department, was the one who made the connection. Donny Easton, the first identified victim, and Gwendolyn Peters, the last, had both attended the same day care. Little Wonders.

Suddenly, the case now had something it had never had before, a legitimate suspect—Frank Guaraldi. And, at the exact same time that Leo was making the connection with the preschool, almost as if by divine intervention, Carolyn Conners, a housewife from College Park, called the tip line and reported a smell like rotting meat coming from the Guaraldis' house. Two detectives interviewed the Conners woman, and she stated to them that she had observed Frank Guaraldi unloading bags of quicklime from the trunk of his car at three o'clock in the morning. She also claimed to have seen Guaraldi remove from his trunk an object wrapped in a plastic tarp. Yes, she had said, although she could not say so definitively, the object wrapped in the tarp could very well have been the body of a child. A search warrant was issued, and Guaraldi and his wife were brought in for questioning. The search of Guaraldi's home yielded a cache of pornographic photographs hidden in a trunk in the attic. The photos depicted, among other things, women in bondage costumes being urinated on by men. Guaraldi's vehicle was impounded. Every print, fiber, and microscopic speck was analyzed in record time. A strand of hair was recovered that matched the DNA of Gwendolyn Peters. Mitigating this was the concurrent discovery of DNA evidence that matched up with nine other (unharmed) attendees of Little Wonders. The Guaraldis denied any knowledge of the missing children. Janice Guaraldi was released from custody and asked to remain available for future questioning. Frank Guaraldi remained behind bars and was held pending formal charges.

In the heat of the media maelstrom that enveloped the city, attorney Monty Lee visited Guaraldi in his cell and offered to take his case pro bono. Guaraldi accepted gratefully and Monty Lee stepped into the limelight for the first time. He called the allegations against his client preposterous and nothing more than just that, allegations. He told the press that his client would sue the county for being held without just cause and being denied due process. The media ignited, and Montgomery Lee became a star.

Letters were drafted by the DA's office and sent out to the parents of children who attended the Little Wonders preschool. The letters asked about any unusual occurrences, inappropriate touching, evidence of violence, and unusual bruising. The children said nothing happened.

At the bail hearing, Leo sat at the prosecution table with Paula, who had been handpicked by the district attorney, Bob Fox, to co-chair the case with Leo. Fox was carefully orchestrating every nuance of the trial. He and everyone else in the city government knew exactly how much was riding on the outcome of this case, and he was leaving nothing to chance. It was fuck or walk, Fox was fond of saying. Fox had told Leo that the positioning of Paula as second chair was a political as well as a practical move. It never hurt to have a pretty woman in court. He firmly believed that having a man and woman sitting at the prosecution table was the only way to go. You had to cover all the bases, after all. And that was certainly true, but it was also true that there was just something about Paula Manning that he simply liked. There was just something about her, something hard underneath.

Fox had entrusted the actual prosecution to Leo because Leo was, after all, the assistant DA and had shepherded all of the evidence thus far to reach this critical point. He believed in Leo. He believed Leo could win the case. He had, after all, given Leo the assistant DA position, hadn't he? Of course he trusted him. Of course he believed in him. Then why did he still have a nagging doubt somewhere in the back of his mind? Leo was one of the best trial lawyers Fox had ever seen, and he was damn glad to have him as his assistant DA, but Leo had yet to show clearly and demonstratively where his loyalties lay. He had not sacrificed. Fox knew that it sometimes took a baptism of fire before some men would totally and completely pledge their loyalties to another man. This would be that time. If the case was won, Fox was sure to go on to become the state attorney general, and the DA's chair would be a fait accompli for Leo.

If the case was lost, all would be lost.

At the bail hearing, Leo addressed the judge in his best tone of placid reason. "Your Honor, in light of the cruel and sadistic nature of the crimes of which Mr. Guaraldi is accused, the People move to deny bail for the defendant," Leo said, and sat back down. Paula, who was sitting to his left, betrayed no emotion.

Guaraldi sat to Monty's left at the defense table. Behind them, Janice Guaraldi waited expectantly. She held a ragged ball of Kleenex in her clenched fist. Behind her, the courtroom was packed with press and the merely curious who wished to know firsthand what sort of bail would be set for the country's most notorious and diabolical child murderer. Monty stood up and nodded imperceptibly to Leo. This was the first time these two men had ever met in or out of court. To Leo, Monty Lee was the high-priced defense attorney who had tried to get Samuel Abdul off the hook. He held Monty Lee in the same contempt as the shiftless lawyer who would have set free the man who had swindled his mother out of her dead husband's inheritance.

"Your Honor, this is outrageous," Monty said with the utmost calm. "My client has committed no crime. He is merely a suspect. And not a very good one at that. We all know that the people of this city live in fear. They demand that the child killer be caught, and rightfully so. The police department, in its clamor to find the killer, to meet the people's demand, has accused the wrong man. In short, the prosecution has yet to offer up one piece of hard evidence. To deny my client bail would be, as I have said, outrageous."

Judge Elizabeth Duran lifted a thick folder and waved it at Monty. Decades of smoking and marinating her vocal cords in single malt scotch had left her voice as deep as a man's. "Mr. Lee, did you read the same police report I did? Two of the missing children were enrolled in his preschool. Did you read the affidavit of the eyewitness who saw your client removing a tarp wrapped in the shape of a body from the trunk of his car? Did you see the same pornographic photographs depicting women being tortured and degraded?"

"Women, Your Honor, not children. A taste for a little S&M isn't a crime."

"No, it's not. However, there's also the matter of the DNA evidence."

"Found along with DNA from nine other children who attend the day care. The Guaraldis often transport the children in that vehicle."

Duran cleared phlegm from her throat and shuffled through the papers one final time.

"I'm sorry, Mr. Lee, but I'm inclined to agree with the

prosecution on this one. I feel that Mr. Guaraldi is a serious threat to the safety of this community, and I would be derelict in my duty to protect this community if I allowed bail."

"But, Your Honor, Mr. Guaraldi has lived in this community for over thirty years, he has no police record, he's never even—"

"I've made my ruling."

"Are you sure Your Honor isn't giving in to the power of the press?"

"That will cost you five hundred dollars. Hope it was worth it. Good day."

A forensics team was brought in to excavate around Guaraldi's house. They dug extensive burrows and tunnels in and around the house. Nothing was found. A backhoe was brought in to excavate the entire property. The same process was carried out at the day care center. Nothing was ever found. Bob Fox was outraged. He set an inhuman pace for his prosecutors. He stormed through offices, demanding results. And Leo didn't blame Fox for demanding results; he knew it was due in large part to the almost daily attacks made on him by the media. In fact, the media were starting to focus some of their attention on Leo, and he didn't like it. Not one bit. Two days after the excavation at Guaraldi's home was abandoned, one of Leo's clerks had buzzed his office and told him he had a call on line two.

"Who is it?" he asked the clerk.

"Anne Hunter."

"Christ. Tell her I'm out of town."

"She says to tell you that she knows you're here and this is going to be your only opportunity to confirm or deny."

"Confirm or deny what?"

"She wouldn't say."

"Christ," he grumbled and punched line two. He had met Anne Hunter shortly after he became a prosecutor. He'd been working on a case involving a minor figure of the community who was suspected in a nonfatal hit-and-run. After court one day, Anne had approached him for comments on the case. He had known that sooner or later he would work on a case that generated some public interest, but he wasn't prepared for the rush he got the first time a reporter actually asked him questions. He felt like a celebrity after the fact. It was ludicrous to feel that way, he knew, but, nonetheless, he got off on it in a big way. It fed his ego. And Anne Hunter had clued in to that right away. She called on him almost daily to get his comments on current cases, cases that he knew were not particularly newsworthy. But it was no big leap for him to talk himself into believing that they were important cases. After all, why would a real reporter want his views on them if they weren't important? But Anne knew what she was doing. They had ultimately ended up seeing each other socially, but once the initial excitement of seeing his name in the paper had worn off, Leo began to dislike her. It had been a bit like going out with a psychiatrist. The conversation always seemed to have a subtext. There was always the feeling that every offhand remark was being neatly filed away and marked for later use. That she was grooming him for her future benefit. And that instinct had been right. Even after the relationship cooled (it had consisted of four sexual encounters and little else), he always called Anne first when he had a story he wanted leaked to the press. And now that he was the ADA on a murder case that had captured the nation's attention, Anne Hunter had the ultimate in. She was reaping the benefits of all the hard work she had put into stroking his ego. Only lately, Anne didn't seem too terribly interested in keeping Leo's ego stroked. Her articles were becoming more and more critical of his performance on the case. Whereas she had once singled out Bob Fox as her whipping boy, she was now targeting Leo. Singling out mistakes he had made. Her last article had used the motif that time was getting short for the children of the city and what were our city's leaders doing about it? The piece had ended with the ominous rejoinder that unless they did something soon, for Bob Fox and Leo Hewitt, as for the children, time was getting short.

"Anne. I'd love to help you with your story, but I'm kinda busy right now. We've got a murder case we're working on. You might have read about it."

"I hear Guaraldi's gonna walk."

"You heard wrong."

"I hear you've got nothing on him. I hear it's gonna be James Nice all over again. You've got what? Two issues of *Teenage Enema Nurses in Bondage?*"

"We've got plenty on Guaraldi."

"That's not what I hear. Come on, Leo, it's only me. Level. Wouldn't you rather *I* broke the story? I'll do it gently. Like always."

"'Time is getting short for Leo Hewitt.' That gently?"

"My sources are very reliable."

"I'm your only source. Look, Anne, it was a nice try. And on the chance that you're not making this up just to trick me into commenting on it, did it ever occur to you that Monty Lee might be generating this rumor to make his client look better? Take it from me, Frank Guaraldi is not going to walk."

"Well I'm running the piece whether you confirm or deny."

"Anne, I just denied it."

"And if it turns out to be true, you'll look—"

"Good-bye, Anne," he said, and hung up on her. She was right about one thing, though. Well, actually, she was right about two things. It was looking more and more like Guaraldi might walk. And, worst of all, time was getting short.

Eventually, even the prosecutors began to lose faith in the case, as did Leo. A roundtable discussion was called by the entire prosecution team, after-hours and without Bob Fox's knowledge. The prosecutors demanded that Leo go to Bob with the suggestion that the charges against Guaraldi be dropped. There was simply no hard evidence against the man. Leo agreed, but first he met with Paula, alone. He had to make one last effort at getting something going before he asked Bob to drop the case and essentially throw away his career. He decided to start at the beginning with the Conners woman and her statements.

"Look, one of the big reasons we kept after Guaraldi was because of the Conners woman. I want to go see her before I ask Bob to drop the charges, which he will never do anyway."

"Do you want me to come?" Paula asked.

"No, I want you to dig up her original call to the tip line. I wanna hear the tape."

Carolyn Conners lived in College Park in an upscale home directly across from the Guaraldi residence. From her front porch, Leo could see the mass of yellow police tape and open craters and what was left of the Guaraldis' once-beautiful home. If we did this to an innocent man, he thought, who was going to take responsibility? Who was going to make it right? He rang the bell. When no one answered, he rang again. A lace curtain hanging in a window off to the side of the house inched open. Leo saw an eye peering out from behind the curtain. The curtain dropped closed, and seconds later a woman opened the front door. She was wearing a hat crudely fashioned from aluminum foil on her head.

"Ms. Conners?"

"Who wants to know?"

Then the smell of her body odor hit him. Rank and foul, the smell of a body months unwashed. He took a step back.

"My name is Leo Hewitt. I'm with the district attorney's office. I'm the assistant DA. I wanted to ask you about what you saw."

"I see a lot. Are you a Democrat?

"Uh, no, I'm not." Behind the woman, Leo could see masses of cats. Hordes of them crawling over tables and chairs.

He saw what could only be feces smeared on the walls. And the smell of the shit and the cats wafted out to him.

"Well, that's good at least, 'cause they been sending agents out here to spy on me. They been sending out transmissions. They put a transmitter in my head, but I block it with the hat."

"Really," Leo said, and began to wish for a cigar.

The prosecution team sat around the conference table. The silence was uncomfortable, and no one would look Leo in the eye.

"You mean to tell me that no one ever just sat down and talked to this woman?"

Paula looked up. "We had her initial statement. The affidavit. We didn't need anything else. She must have seemed lucid at the—"

"Lucid!" Leo growled. "She's fucking Boo Radley on acid! I have to go into Bob's office and tell him that we practically bulldozed this guy's house into the ground—into the *ground*—based on the accusations of a lunatic!"

"It gets worse," Paula said, and opened her briefcase.

She laid a series of audiocassettes on the table.

"What are those?"

"Remember you wanted her original call? Well, they fed her name into the system and pulled every call she ever made to the hotline. There were over fifty."

"What? You're kidding, right? Tell me you're kidding."

"I haven't had time to listen to all the tapes, but in each call she accuses another suspect."

"I just don't understand why this was ever taken seriously."

"It was just an unlucky coincidence. If you remember, Bob demanded that every call be followed up on, no matter what. It was just a coincidence that the call in which she names Guaraldi came in at the same time we started looking at Guaraldi because of the Peters and Easton children. Any other time, the call would have been tagged as a nutcase, but because Guaraldi was being investigated by us at the time, someone took the call seriously. It was just a coincidence."

"Just a coincidence. Christ."

Bob stared at the stack of tapes on his desk.

"Has defense heard them?"

"No. Not yet." Leo stood in front of Bob, felt the rage coming off the man like a fever. Paula stood off to the left.

"Not yet? What do you mean, not yet?"

"I figured you'd want to hear them first."

"You're goddamn right I do. But we are not, let me repeat that, we are *not* giving these tapes to the defense."

"It's discovery. We have no choice."

"Sure we do. Bury the tapes. Lose them. Erase them. I never heard of these tapes. Paula lost them before she got a chance to listen to them. Right, Paula?"

"Yeah. Sure, Bob."

"We'll put the woman on the stand," Bob said.

"Look, I'm telling you, she's a basket case. She wears a hat made out of Reynolds Wrap!"

"We'll shoot her full of Thorazine! One way or another, she's going on the stand."

"Bob, think about what you're saying. We've got nothing on Guaraldi. Nothing."

"We've got one of the dead girls' DNA in the man's car. DNA. You call that nothing?"

"It's diluted. It has no value. There's blood, spit, prints, and hair from nine of the day-care kids in that car. All alive."

"All but one."

"This is ludicrous."

"No, Leo, this is critical mass. It's fuck or walk. Where do your loyalties lie?"

The two men stared at each other like tyrants on a playground. Leo looked to Paula for some backup, but she was of no help. She had, quite clearly, shown where her loyalties lay.

Leo picked up the tapes off Bob's desk. "Bob, the case is over. It's over."

Bob jumped to his feet so quickly and violently that Leo had been sure the man was going to hit him. His face had gone from an angry red color to an apoplectic purple. "Like hell it is. Put those goddamn tapes back on my desk."

"Look, you're not thinking clearly. We can't put a man

who's obviously innocent in prison just so your résumé will remain unblemished."

"You had best think about what you're doing here, Leo. I would hate to see you ruin what could be a brilliant career. Think about it. You know he's innocent? You *know?*"

"It doesn't matter. We don't have a case against the man. I'm turning these tapes over to the defense team. They're discovery. We're legally obligated."

"No, we're not. They have the same access to the hotline tapes as we do. We are not legally obligated to give them something that they in fact already have."

"It's wrong and you know it."

"We are not legally obligated."

"We're morally obligated."

"Fuck morally! Fuck you! Give me those tapes!" Bob lunged across his desk and grabbed at Leo. He got hold of the cuff of Leo's suit jacket, and Leo jerked away, tearing the jacket. Leo backed slowly away from Bob, who was sprawled out across his desk, a thin thread of saliva dangling from his chin. "If you walk out of this office, that's it! I never want to see you again!"

"You won't. I quit."

After listening to the tapes, Judge Duran ordered the charges dropped. Frank Guaraldi was set free and Monty filed a seventy-million-dollar civil action lawsuit on Guaraldi's behalf for wrongful imprisonment. Bob Fox held a press conference that culminated with his stating that in the wake of his monumental mishandling of the Guaraldi case, Assistant District Attorney Leo Hewitt had voluntarily resigned his position. This statement was interpreted, as Fox knew it would be, that Leo was forced to leave. The media, and more important, the voters, accepted Leo as the scapegoat and Fox was ultimately reelected for another term as district attorney and named Paula Manning as his assistant DA.

Leo lived well with his decision to turn over the Conners tapes. He knew his actions were appropriate.

Two months after being acquitted of all charges, Frank Guaraldi was stopped late at night for a routine traffic violation. The patrolman deemed Guaraldi's behavior suspicious. As the neighborhood in which he had stopped Guaraldi was notorious for high drug trafficking, the patrolman searched Guaraldi's car. He found nothing in the interior of the car and asked Guaraldi to pop the trunk. Guaraldi ran. The officer caught him easily and restrained him with handcuffs. He opened the trunk of Guaraldi's car. Inside he found the limbless, headless torso of a seven-year-old girl.

Guaraldi was taken into custody and retried. Paula headed the prosecution team, and there was no doubt that Guaraldi would be convicted, but he never was.

Late one night in his jail cell, Guaraldi tore open his wrists with his own teeth, biting and tearing the flesh until he reached the artery and severed it. He jammed his wrists into an open toilet and quietly bled to death in his cell in the middle of the night, and thus saved the taxpayers of the city the cost of another trial.

Leo succumbed to depression and felt that he was responsible for the death of the last child. He could not find a job anywhere in the country (much less Fulton County), and a brief attempt at a private practice proved to be a folly. Even the most desperate of clients felt that they could do better than the man who had set a child murderer free. He grew poor and found that he missed having money. He took a low-rent apartment in a bad neighborhood. When the lease expired on his Lexus, he purchased a used Nissan pickup truck. He fell into the habit of driving through tony neighborhoods and dreaming of the prosperity that being a successful trial lawyer might have brought him. He imagined what might have happened had he destroyed the Conners tapes as Bob had suggested. He could see himself as the district attorney. He could see himself resigning the position to accept a full partnership in a prestigious law firm. The reality was that he took a job as a data entry clerk. He showed up every day and pushed buttons on a keyboard and dreamed his dreams. The job was functional and paid the rent, but the law was all he knew, all he had ever cared to know.

One day, he went to the criminal courts building and hid out in the parking garage. When Paula spotted him waiting near her car, her eyes widened and she reached into her purse. Leo was sure she was reaching for a can of mace, but she only pulled out her keys. She opened the car door and told Leo to get in. Without shame, he begged her to help him get back. To go to Bob and somehow get him back in. She agreed.

Two weeks later Paula contacted him. She had talked to Bob. He would take Leo back. As a junior deputy prosecutor. Traffic cases only. Take it or leave it.

He took it.

TWENTY-FOUR

"Leo, please, Mr. Lee. Just Leo."

"And I'm Adam. How can I help you?"

"This is a hell of a nice office, Adam. Is that desk mahogany?"

"Yes. How can I help you?"

"Well, Adam, the thing is, I thought you were going to have Ms. Perkins call me."

"Yes, I was. I've been unable to contact Violet. I tried, but her number has been disconnected. It was a, uh, one-night-stand type of thing. I'm sure you understand."

"Oh, I understand perfectly. We've all been there, right? Hey, I like that suit. Armani, right?"

"Yes, Armani."

"Mine's just an off-the-rack job, but not too bad, huh?"

"No, it's quite dapper."

Leo could sense Adam tensing up, not sure if he should tell this short little bald man to get the fuck out of his office. Leo loved playing the cat-and-mouse game. It felt good. He liked being the cat. He liked the look of terror in the mouse's eyes. He liked letting the mouse think he'd lost interest, then pouncing on him and starting the game anew.

"Yeah, we've all been there. One-nighters. But you were with her the entire weekend?"

"Yes, just as I told you earlier. I was under the impression that this matter was closed. It was a tragedy. I am still in mourning. I'm afraid that I can't quite see how bringing my marital indiscretions into the light will deepen anyone's understanding of a senseless death."

It felt good to have a little power again. Leo wished for a cigar to top off this extraordinary sensation, this exhilarating rush of the kill. It had been so long. He was on top of his game like never before. This cheap prick in his thousand-dollar suit was easy prey.

"Of course not, but as I said earlier, I have to verify your story in order to close the file. Do you happen to remember where you first met Violet?"

"At the Hendrix Institute."

"Where your son stays?"

"I'm sorry, Mr. Hewitt, but I'm a busy man. I don't see the point to this. Am I under some sort of suspicion?"

"Well, actually, Mr. Lee, there have been some irregularities in the case. Certain inconsistencies."

"Inconsistencies?"

"I don't believe your son killed your wife."

"You don't?"

"No, I don't. And because of this I'm going to have to verify your whereabouts that weekend. And I'm going to have to speak to Violet Perkins."

"I see. Perhaps I should call my brother."

"Perhaps you should."

In the lobby of the Lawson Building, Leo stepped off the elevator and lit a cigar. When he looked up, he saw a painting of Rachel's father, Benjamin Lawson. It was a massive oil on canvas framed in pewter. His date of birth and date of death were inscribed on a bronze plaque under the portrait.

TWENTY-FIVE

Adam parked his car in the macadam lot of the Hendrix Institute. He walked alone under the sodium arc lights. Inside, he tried to remain matter-of-fact with the desk nurse. He didn't want to betray his urgency. He had foreseen no reason to contact Violet after their last weekend together, and now found that he couldn't locate her. Apparently, she didn't want to be located.

"I'm really sorry, Mr. Lee."

"Perhaps she quit."

"It's possible, but I've been here seven years and I've never heard of her. I make out the schedules."

"And Violet is a somewhat unusual name. You'd remember a name like Violet."

"Yes, I'd remember. I'm sorry."

* * *

Cigar smoke, thick and acrid, floated from the open window of Leo's pickup truck. He watched Adam leave the building and drive away.

The next day, Adam met Monty for lunch. They took their sandwiches from the greasy-haired man behind the deli counter. All the tables were jammed full with the lunch hour crowd. The two brothers stood at the counter and ate. Monty wolfed his down and talked around the food in his mouth.

"He's a loser. He just wants to make himself look good."

"He keeps calling me. He came to my office."

"He's a kiss-ass. When I couldn't get down there that night, he says, 'Oh, Mr. Lee, I'd be happy to go make sure your brother's all right.' Now he's just trying to impress his boss, whom, by the way, I've fucked."

Adam wrapped his half-eaten sandwich in a napkin and tossed it in the trash.

"He says I need an alibi for that weekend. That there are inconsistencies."

"Inconsistencies? Inconsistencies? That fat bald fuck. Look, I'll call up Paula, maybe let her suck my dick, give her a good fuck. She'll tell the loser, this Leo, to drown his sorrows in a glass of . . . Slim Fast, and leave you the fuck alone. Trust me. I'll take care of you."

Monty popped the last of the sandwich into his mouth, finishing it in one huge bite.

TWENTY-SIX

Leo waited outside the courtroom and wished for a cigar. He hated being down here. People still recognized him from before. Other lawyers. Within his profession, and to some degree outside it, he was infamous. And down here, around the criminal courts, his presence was apt to draw stares. He might as well have a placard around his neck—*I'm the man who set a child killer free.* And as much as he hated being down here, this was where he wanted to be. This was where he knew he could soar. If he could somehow parlay this Lee thing into a second chance, he wasn't going to waste it. He knew it would be his only chance. And he knew there was something there. Something wrong. And if he could convince Paula, and Paula could convince Bob . . .

A man reading from a legal pad slowed down as he passed by Leo and looked him over.

"Got a problem, buddy?"

The man looked away and continued on his way across the lobby. Leo stared after the man and thought back to the kinder, gentler days when sand-filled ashtrays dotted this lobby. A cigar would be nice right about now.

The doors of the courtroom swung open and a crowd of people exited the courtroom and filled up the lobby. Among them, he spotted Paula heading briskly toward the elevators.

"Paula!"

Leo ran to catch up with her and followed a few steps behind her.

"Leo! Find anything on the grassy knoll?"

"Well, nothing to speak of."

"Speak of it."

"Well, like you said, the kid did the same thing five years ago. I call him a kid, but have you seen him? He's a bruiser. Anyway, they put him away after he cracks Mom's head open the first time. Then a year later he kills another mentally retarded man in the hospital arguing over socks. Called it an accident. So they put him in this Hendrix Institute, private, high dollar, and strictly for the hard-core types. Are you with me?"

Paula quickened the pace a little to try to get to an open elevator before it closed. "Keep going."

"And so here we are now and the husband decides it's

time for a little home visit about the same time he decides to go away with Princess Di for a romantic weekend getaway." He followed Paula onto the crowded elevator.

"They let the kid out? With a history like that?"

"Like I said. Private. High dollar. Albert has never been charged with a crime."

"And Princess Di?"

"She's some kind of nurse at the institute. Very discreet, huh? So Mom's at home with the Incredible Hulk and Daddy's in the mountains getting his candle waxed, and then uh-oh, the kid cracks Mom in the head again. Only this time she's dead."

"And what you're trying to say is?"

Leo waited until the elevator stopped. They got off and headed for Paula's office.

"I don't think Junior iced Mom."

"Because . . ."

"Number one, the murderer's left-handed, the kid's right. Number two, we got blood splatters on the drapes, on the walls, the place looks like *Helter Skelter* and there's not a drop on the kid."

"You know, I saw the pictures. It wasn't *that* bad."

"But still."

Paula opened her office with a key. She tossed the keys on top of the coffeemaker, plopped into her chair, kicked off her shoes, and propped her legs on the desk.

"The father probably cleaned the kid up before you got

there. He might have found the sight of his child covered with his wife's blood somewhat disturbing. I think you're seeing something because you want to see something."

"I talked to the husband. He smells guilty."

"Okay. He smells guilty. I'm going to need a little more than that. A jury will, too. The kid's fingerprints are still all over the ashtray, right? The ashtray with half of Rachel Lee's scalp stuck in the grooves."

"'Hey Junior, hold this ashtray for Daddy.' The kid is retarded, don't forget. It wouldn't be terribly difficult to frame him."

"Think about it, Leo. There's no motive. No why. Why? That's what I'm not seeing. If you could give me a why, I might be able to buy into some of this other stuff. He's not even in line for the inheritance. The wife left it all to the son. The insurance on her wouldn't even move the decimal point in this guy's checkbook."

Paula opened her top desk drawer and pulled out a pack of cigarettes and an ashtray. Leo leaned across the desk, lighted her cigarette, then fired up his cigar.

"Like old times, huh, Paula?"

"Sure. I remember."

"Working late, excited about a case, smoking like maniacs. We used to work good together."

"You taught me a lot. I haven't forgotten. You taught me to look out for myself. And that's what I've been doing."

"Yeah, I know."

"Look, I want to see something good happen for you. I

do. But I don't think this is the one. It all comes back to the why. You can't convince a jury without the why. 'He did it, oh yes, he definitely did it. Why? Well, I'm not sure why, but—?'"

"Okay, I get the point. All right, let's say, what if—now I'm not saying anything, but what if *she* was having an affair?"

"The woman hadn't set foot out of her house in three years."

"The postman always rings twice."

"He'd have to ring more than that before this psycho would answer the door."

Paula pulled a thick folder from a drawer and tossed it across the desk to Leo.

"Have you read her file? Depression, anxiety, agoraphobia. Taking Valium and Prozac by the handful."

Leo picked up the file. The significance of her giving it to him was not lost on him. *She's giving it to me,* he thought. *The case. This is my case. She's not just letting me stick my nose in to get a little whiff of what it used to be like, she's giving it to me.*

"Take it home, read it over. You'll see you're just jumping at shadows. The woman makes Boo Radley look like an extrovert."

Boo Radley. Who had they used to call Boo Radley? It was right there. It was . . . the Conners woman.

"Crazier than Carolyn Conners?"

"Carolyn Conners?"

"Like you forgot."

Neither of them had mentioned the Guaraldi case in front of the other since Leo had been back with the DA's office. But there it was. As he had hoped, Paula acted nonchalant, and he knew everything would be okay.

"Oh. Carolyn Conners. I'd have to say that this woman could have probably given Carolyn Conners a run for her money. Psychotically speaking, that is."

"Not a very nice way to speak of the dead, but maybe you have something."

"What?"

"Psycho. I'm not saying anything, but maybe she was so crazy, maybe he knew she'd never give him a divorce. Maybe he was afraid of her."

"*I'd* be scared of her. Tell me more."

"Maybe he knew she'd never let him leave. Maybe there was only one way for him to get his life back."

"Kill her."

"I'm not saying anything."

"This is good. This I can see. This is motive. But we can't convict someone because they're left-handed or because they smell guilty. We'll need evidence. Hard evidence. A fingerprint. Bloodstains. Skin traces under the nails."

"How about a witness?"

"A witness would be good. Have you got one?"

Leo opened his mouth to speak, but Paula cut him off.

"I know. You're not saying anything."

TWENTY-SEVEN

Monty lifted his head from between Paula's parted legs. He gauged the level of ecstasy in her glazed-over eyes, decided he could do better, and began to use his teeth. Her back began to arch, and she grabbed his head roughly with her hands, pushed his face deeper into her. She cried out, and Monty knew that he had succeeded.

Later, he lit a cigarette for each of them and put the ashtray on his chest for her to use.

"Adam asked me to talk to you about Leo."

"Leo's harmless. I'm just giving the dog a bone."

"Adam seems nervous."

"You want Leo gone? He's gone. Believe me, I have him on a very short leash. I was just letting him play lawyer, for old

times' sake. You have no idea how embarrassing it is to see
him groveling. Pathetic."

"No, let him play. I don't care."

"You don't?"

"No. Adam's not acting right. He's changed somehow.
Frankly, I'd like to know what he's been up to. I mean, I don't
think he had anything to do with Rachel's death, but I would
be very interested to know what kind of trash Leo can dig up.
I wouldn't mind knowing for myself who he was with that
weekend."

"Your wish is my command."

TWENTY-EIGHT

"You want to drag your brother into it, that's fine by me. I'll be just as happy to talk to him. But I gotta tell you, it's just gonna make you look that much more suspicious."

"Suspicious? I've done nothing wrong! You know that."

"Look, we can play it any way you want to, Mr. Lee, I'm just trying to give you a break."

"Harassing me at my office is your idea of giving me a break? This is turning into a nightmare and you are the bogeyman."

"Look, I said from the beginning I was gonna have to talk to her. You assured me it wouldn't be a problem. It was gonna just be between us. Well, it's been two weeks since your wife died and still no Violet Perkins."

"I don't know why she hasn't contacted you. She assured me she would."

"Why don't you give me her number? I'll call her."

"I told you, she calls me. She doesn't have a phone."

"Look, I think we both know Violet Perkins doesn't exist. At least that's the way it's starting to look. I've located four Violet Perkinses in the metro area, and I've talked to all of them except one. Two of them were grade school students, another was living in a nursing home, and the last one has been dead for seven months. The Hendrix Institute denies any knowledge of her. In fact, only one person can claim to have seen her—you."

Adam pushed back his chair, stood, and looked out his office window. After a minute, he turned back around to look at Leo. "She exists. Look, Leo, I admit I've been lying. I haven't had contact with her since that weekend. We more or less ended the affair. That weekend was the coup de grâce. Don't you think I want to find her just as much as you do? It's my name, my reputation on the line."

Adam faced away from Leo, turned back to the window. Leo smiled. The mouse trembles, and the cat licks beads of blood from its whiskers.

When the desk nurse didn't look up from her charting, Leo cleared his throat a little louder. She looked up, mildly annoyed at being interrupted.

"Hi, my name is Leo Hewitt. I'm with the district attorney's office. I was wondering if you could help me. I'm looking for a Violet Perkins. I've already been to administration twice, but I thought I could check down here, too, just in case."

"Oh, yeah. There was a guy in here the other day. Looking for the same girl. I remember 'cause of the name. Violet. I told him I been here for years, never heard of her."

Leo sighed and turned away. "Well, thanks anyway."

"Then I happened to think. Maybe I didn't know her because she's not on regular staff."

"What do you mean?"

"We hire out to a temp agency when we're short on staff, which is all the time. Payroll cuts a check directly to the company and they pay their employees from their end; the person's name never goes on our payroll. And when I fill in the schedules, I just pencil in the word *temp* because I never know who they'll be sending over."

"Is that a fact?"

The nurse cracked open her Rolodex and flipped through it. She scribbled a number on a scrap of paper and shoved it across the counter at Leo.

"BWB Temporary Services. Check with them."

"Thanks, I will."

Leo folded the paper over and inserted it into his breast pocket.

Halfway down the directory posted in the lobby of the building, Leo found BWB Temporary Services. He took the elevator to the ninth floor and introduced himself to a good-looking, youngish man eating a take-out sandwich at his cluttered desk.

"It must be exciting working for the DA's office."

"You'd be surprised."

"I guess that was a stupid thing to say. I bet everybody says that. It's probably boring just like everybody else's job. Although I can personally testify that running a temp agency is never boring. Every day there's another emergency. Some girl's got her period and can't work her assignment. Some boy's got *his* period and won't come in. You know how it is."

"The thing is, I'm looking for a lady who might have worked for you."

"What's her name?"

"Violet Perkins."

"Oh sure, Violet worked for us."

"She did?"

"Sure."

"I've been looking all over for her. I was beginning to think she didn't exist."

"Oh, she exists all right. But she's not on my Christmas list, I can tell you that much. I had an assignment for her three weeks ago and she never showed. You have no idea what a bad impression it makes when one of our people is a no-show. The clients usually don't call back. Anyway, I bet you ran her name through your computer and couldn't find her."

"Right."

"I bet I know why."

"Why?"

"Because you were right, she doesn't exist. Her name isn't Violet. It's Constance. That's what it says on her driver's license. But she hates it, so she tells everybody to call her Violet. And I have to say, I don't blame her. Violet is much more colorful. I've got a photocopy of it if you want."

"What?"

"Her driver's license. We have to keep one on file for everybody that works here."

The youngish man, Leo could now see, augmented his good looks with a bit of makeup and was older than he had first thought. He opened a massive filing cabinet drawer and thumbed through the files until he got to the right one. He held out a photocopied page to Leo.

"Here, you can keep it. Since she doesn't work here anymore, I won't be needing it."

"I really appreciate this. You don't know how much."

"Happy to help."

"So, what does BWB stand for? I guess everybody asks."

"Everybody does, and I always say they're my mother's initials, but for you, I'll tell the truth. When Craig, that's my partner, when we started the business, it was just the two of us. And it was just a cleaning service. We went into rich people's homes and cleaned up. And we really did—clean up, that is. So we expanded into other areas and hired more people and eventually became a multiservice temp agency. We just never bothered to change our name, which has since grown to be an embarrassment."

"Because?"

"Because BWB stands for Bitches With Brooms."

TWENTY-NINE

"This is Anne Hunter, may I help you?"

"Guess who's investigating a murder at the DA's office?"

"Who is this?"

"Do you want the story or not? Maybe I should call Dear Abby."

"Okay, spill it."

"The man who set the Torso Killer free is working a murder case."

"Leo Hewitt? Investigating a murder? That's not possible. What murder?"

"Rachel Lee."

"Look, why don't you give me your—"

Anne heard the click of the line disengaging and hung up the phone. She took a notepad from her desk and wrote:

Leo Hewitt, Rachel Lee, possible connection with Monty Lee? She looked at the paper a moment, then added: *This has got to be bullshit!*

Anne Hunter had been the first to break the story about the infighting in the DA's office during the Guaraldi trial. She'd coined the term every paper in the nation picked up on: *The Guaraldi Fiasco.* Even the television news shows used it. And it had been the headline of her first lead story: The Guaraldi Fiasco. And thanks to her source on the prosecution team, she had scooped every paper in the nation—as well as television and radio—with Hewitt's resignation. But then, Hewitt himself had been her source. Who was Mr. Anonymous that had just called her? He had to work in the DA's office to get that kind of information. If it was true. It would be nice to write another lead story; the only problem was that once Leo had his fall from grace, no one at the DA's office would talk to her. She'd pretty much burned those bridges. And, truth be told, she'd had something of a hand in Leo's undoing. Her stories had targeted the entire DA's office for its mishandling of key evidence, and, at the end, she had singled out Leo for her tirades.

Her last story on the case had been an overview of Leo Hewitt's legal career and had been titled, *The Man Who Set the Torso Killer Free.* The story had, in effect, bordered on slander but got her on the short list for the Pulitzer that year. And the woman who had once been as close to a Pulitzer as Roxanne's trumpet was now covering county zoning meetings. And here she was, wondering if that far-off whistle was the sound of the gravy train pulling back into the station. Maybe it sounded too good to be true, but she'd be a fool not to follow up on it. She picked up the phone and dialed. The number was still as fresh in her mind as it had been three years ago.

"This is Anne Hunter with the *Tribune.* Put me through to Paula Manning's office."

She listened to a series of electronic clicks, then heard the phone ringing on Paula's secretary's desk.

"Hi, this is Anne Hunter with the *Tribune.* I need to speak with Paula. I know she's not in, but while you're checking to make sure she's not in, please tell her I'm running a story on the Lee case and this will be her only opportunity to confirm or deny. I'll hold."

She waited for several minutes, and the next voice she heard was Paula's.

"There is no Lee case. What are you talking about, Anne?"

"Rachel Lee. Your office is investigating her death."

The line was silent, and Anne knew she'd screwed up. She should have at least confirmed that someone named Rachel Lee had died recently. She could kick herself for being so stupid. She closed her eyes and hoped for the best. Maybe Paula would trip herself up.

"I don't know what you heard, but it's wrong."

Bull's-eye. "I hear that you have Leo Hewitt working the case. And Paula, I got this from a very reliable source in your own department. I'm running the story whether you confirm it or deny it, but if you do deny it, you're gonna look like either a liar or an incompetent who doesn't know what's going on in her own office. Either way, you're gonna look bad."

"Well, that's your specialty, isn't it? Making people look bad. It was a nice try, but you can't bluff me, Anne. If you really had a source that strong, the last thing you would do is call me."

"I'm not bluffing. Try me."

"You're way out of line on this. First of all, the district attorney's office is not investigating the death of Rachel Lee. It was deemed an accident. Second, Leo Hewitt works traffic court. You get the picture?"

"Yeah, I get it. Hey, you can't blame a girl for trying, right?"

"Look, Anne, just between me and you, do you honestly think Bob Fox would let Leo Hewitt investigate a cat up a tree? Someone's pulling your leg."

Anne hung up the phone. She knew Paula was right, of course. The whole thing was ludicrous. The only problem was, if the whole thing was just a joke, Paula would never have taken her call.

Anne closed the notepad and stuck it in her purse, put the purse over her shoulder, and headed for the door. Before she could get out the door, she was ambushed by her editor, Jack Jones, whose massive bulk completely blocked the doorway.

"You finished that piece on the rezoning committee meeting?"

"It's on your desk."

"It wasn't five minutes ago."

"A lot can happen in five minutes, as I'm sure your wife is well aware."

"You know what you are, Hunter? You're friendly. That goddamn piece had better be on my desk."

"What if I told you I might have a possible story on Leo Hewitt?"

"I'd still want the rezoning story."

"What if I said they put him on another murder case?"

"Fuck the rezoning. What have you got?"

THIRTY

"Paula, you busy?"

"Do I look busy?" Paula asked, covering the mouthpiece of the phone cradled between her chin and neck. "Let me call you back," she said to whoever was on the other end and hung up the phone. She crooked her finger at Leo and said, "Actually, come in, I need to talk to you."

"Good, I need to talk to you about something, too."

"Look, Leo, I was happy to let you dig around a little with this Lee thing. Who knows, you might find something we missed, right? But it's got to stop. Right now. Officially, there is no case. There never was. I want you to let it alone."

"Are you sure about that?"

"Of course I'm sure. I don't know who you've been talk-

145

ing to, or what kind of impression you're giving people, but this was never your case. There was never a case, period."

"Did something happen?"

"Yes, something happened. That Hunter bitch had the nerve to call me."

"Anne Hunter?"

"Do you know another one? She has somehow gotten the impression you're working a murder case. Any idea how that could have happened? Do you miss the old glory so much that you'd put my ass on the line to see your name in the paper again?"

"Anne Hunter is no friend of mine. She crucified me in the press. You know that."

"The thing is, if this gets in the papers, Bob is going to come gunning for me for going behind his back. It all stops now."

"Sure, whatever you say, Paula. But before I leave, I've got someone here I'd like you to meet."

Leo opened the door wider and ushered in a young woman in a white sundress.

"Paula Manning, I'd like you to meet Violet Perkins. Violet has something she'd like to tell you."

THIRTY-ONE

Monty found himself staring at the phone again. He was waiting for the call that he knew would come. Paula had called several hours before and told him that Adam would be taken into custody tonight. On some level, Monty knew that all of this was inevitable.

While he waited for the call, he was watching an old black-and-white movie on television. It helped distract his mind from the disturbing fact that his brother would soon be arrested for murder. The black-and-white images on the television screen flickered seductively in front of him. He remembered when he and Adam used to stay up all night in their basement kingdom watching old movies. *Out of the Past. Criss Cross. The Treasure of the Sierra Madre.* Anything swift and violent. He learned from these movies in a way Adam had not. He incorporated their vision into his vision. He learned that greed, the unyielding need to possess what other men already possessed, was the driving force in most men's lives. He took this knowledge and transformed it into a successful legal career. This same knowledge seemed to be too much for Adam. It burdened him until the weight became too much and Adam collapsed in on himself like a black hole. He became a cipher, a negative. A desperate man leading a desperate life.

Monty was watching *Double Indemnity*. Fred MacMurray and Barbara Stanwyck had just killed Barbara Stanwyck's husband and thrown his body off a moving train to make it look like an accident, but Monty knew that they would be caught. For one thing, there was Edward G. Robinson. There was always someone like Edward G. Robinson hanging around to catch you. No matter how smart you were, no matter how perfectly you had planned the murder, Edward G. Robinson was always smarter, always one step ahead. Plus, you could never trust the woman. Barbara Stanwyck would always betray you in the end. She was always hiding something. She was never what she seemed. In fact, it looked as though the only way to get away with murder was to accept from the beginning that Edward G. Robinson was going to catch you, and Barbara Stanwyck was going to betray you and then, maybe, just maybe, you might have a fighting chance of getting away with it.

Monty knew this to be true. He wondered if Adam did.

Even if Adam did know these things to be true, Monty was sure the lesson would be lost on him.

He watched the movie and waited for the phone to ring.

The doorbell chimed and Adam paused a minute before switching off the television. He had been watching *Double Indemnity* on Turner Classic Movies. It was almost over and he wanted to see his favorite part before he answered the door and stepped into the next phase of his life. The film had been one of his favorites since childhood. One he and Monty had watched late one night in their underground realm, each of them enthralled in the dark drama that played out before them in flickering, staccato pulses of light.

Adam had discovered that the movie offered a valuable lesson for the careful viewer. It was a lesson that he doubted Monty had ever learned. The lesson: Women were inherently dangerous. Adam knew this to be true; hadn't his life thus far proven it to be so? Yes, women were inherently dangerous, but of course one couldn't shun their company for a lifetime. One needed only to accept this fact and act accordingly. Don't tempt fate. Adam had selected just one woman, but, given the theorem that all women were a risky proposition, it had not necessarily been his fault that his chosen one had been so badly damaged. And when the time had come to select a second woman, had he not made a better choice? Had he not had the upper hand? Did he not succeed in controlling her true nature, her inherent danger? Yes, he had made two careful selections in one lifetime, but Monty, Monty wallowed in women. He used them to excess. He did not understand their dangerous nature. The lesson had been lost on him. Adam knew that his brother's beauty had shielded him from much of that danger, but soon, the odds would catch up with him. The threat would come back on him twofold.

Adam watched now as Fred MacMurray finally learned the lesson, finally acknowledged Barbara Stanwyck's inherent danger and sought to save himself from her. He shot Barbara Stanwyck. But not before she shot him. Yes, he had finally learned the lesson, and the knowledge had only cost him his life.

The doorbell rang again, and Adam turned off the television and wondered if all those years ago, he and Monty had been watching the same movie.

He opened the door without first checking to see who was there. He knew who was on the other side. The door swung open to reveal Leo, dressed in his best ready-to-wear suit, a cigar clamped between his teeth. Behind him, two uniformed policemen stood framed in the doorway.

He let them in without speaking. As one of the officers read him his Miranda rights, Leo stood off to the side watching the drama unfold. The glee in Leo's eyes as the ritual was carried out was unmistakable and at the same time unnerving. Adam wouldn't have thought the pudgy little bald man would have been capable of such serene happiness.

"Do you understand these rights as I've read them to you?"

"I understand."

Leo stepped forward and handed Adam a legal paper. It was a search warrant. Leo asked Adam to sign the warrant and Adam complied. There was nothing to be found in the house, perhaps baubles that would ignite the little man's jealousy, but nothing Adam did not want to be found.

"May I make a phone call now?"

"Yeah, go ahead."

Adam lifted the receiver and dialed. He found that his fingers were having trouble finding the buttons but, in the end, they did not betray him. He listened to the faint ringing on the other end. Then the click of the receiver being picked up and Monty's expectant voice.

"I need you. They're here."

THIRTY=TWO

BROTHER DEFENDS BROTHER

by Anne Hunter

staff writer

Adam Lee, brother of criminal defense attorney Montgomery Lee, was arrested in his home in the upscale Peachtree Battle neighborhood of East Atlanta. Adam Lee is charged with the murder of his wife, Rachel Lee. Mrs. Lee's body was discovered by her husband Oct. 3 in their home. Mrs. Lee died as a result of repeated blows to the head. It was initially believed these fatal blows were inflicted by the couple's mentally retarded son, Albert Lee, who has a history of violent behavior. Montgomery Lee, in a move that many legal analysts call highly unusual, is defending his brother. Neither brother could be reached for comment. Also highly unusual, it has been reported that Leo Hewitt will be handling the prosecution for the district attorney's office. Mr. Hewitt gained notoriety three years ago for his mishandling of key evidence in the trial of child killer Frank Guaraldi. Mr. Guaraldi was subsequently freed only to be caught less than a month later with the corpse of a young girl. The district attorney's office denies any involvement of Mr. Hewitt in the Lee case.

Bob Fox crumpled up the paper and tossed it in the wastebasket. "Un-fucking-believable. What were you thinking, Paula?"

"Anne Hunter doesn't have a clue as to what goes on in this office. I let Leo ask a couple of questions on my behalf."

"A couple of questions?"

"What can I say? I'm just an old softy. He asked me what I was working on, and I told him about the case I was building against Lee. He begged me to let him help out. What could I say?"

"Judging from past experience, you should have said no."

"You're right. I'm sorry."

"Ahh, hell, Paula, I don't care if you gave Leo a taste. We can't hold him down forever. But I've got to be totally honest with you. What distresses me is that you went behind my back on this thing."

"I know."

Paula sat across from Fox in his office. His neatly trimmed, nearly white hair, in addition to his name, had earned him from the press the nickname "the Silver Fox."

"I want you to know that the effort you've put into this case hasn't gone unnoticed. Yes, I know, it's time to forgive and forget, but one thing you must never forget is who you work for."

"You're right."

"I know I'm right." His career was only now beginning to recover from the blemish of Leo Hewitt and the Guaraldi fiasco. The fact that Leo had never gone public with Bob's refusal to admit the hotline tapes of the Conners woman into evidence was not lost on Bob Fox. He was well aware that Leo could have told the press that Fox had demanded that the tapes be illegally destroyed. These little facts had tempered his view of Leo. Leo had accepted his role of scapegoat. Of course, had he gone to the media with tales of wrongdoings and dirty deeds, Bob would simply have denied any knowledge of the tapes and Paula would have backed him up, because Paula was a team player and Paula knew where to stake her loyalties, which was why Paula was sitting across from him now. But Leo's willingness to take the burden of blame was not lost on Bob. The wounds had healed, and retrospect showed that there was blame enough for everybody. Of course, Leo could never again be given a position of trust, but he was willing to let the man be forgiven, and if Paula wanted the same thing, he'd give it to her.

"You made this case, and I know it. Who do you want backing you up in court? Anybody you want."

"Anybody?"

"Name your man. If Leo's who you want, just say so. I defer to your judgment. I told you, I'm ready to forgive and forget."

Paula thought carefully before she spoke, her mouth drawn into a tight, neat line. "I'm not. I can forgive, but I can't forget. I don't believe Leo can be trusted. Sure, he makes a fine errand boy when I'm building a case, but I want someone I can trust backing me up in the courtroom. You say name my man? Okay. I name you."

THIRTY-THREE

In the interview room, Adam sat at the bare table and watched through the wire-reinforced glass windows as guards and visitors walked by. One of the guards, a blank-faced hulk of a man with tattoos crawling up his meaty forearms, unlocked the door and held it open for Monty. Monty walked in under the guard's arm and tossed his briefcase across the table.

"I've got an in with the judge's clerk, and it looks certain bail will be denied. You need to prepare yourself for that. I could scream and yell, but it might be smarter to just roll over, stay in the judge's good graces. This thing will get some news play, so bottom line is it's political.

"Political or not, I just don't understand why I am here at all."

"Apparently the DA's office has got some pretty damning evidence against you."

"How could there be evidence against me? There is no evidence. There is no crime."

"Does the name Constance Perkins mean anything to you?"

"Constance?"

"Also known as Violet."

"Oh."

"Oh? What the fuck do you mean, 'Oh'? Look, Adam, it's time to fess up. Who is Violet Perkins?"

"I had an affair with her. I told them that."

"Told who?"

"Leo Hewitt."

"Goddamn! I should never have called that fucking sawed-off prick."

"So what do I do?"

"There's nothing. You have to wait. For the trial. I'm sorry. They're not gonna allow bail."

"So I have to stay in jail. What am I going to do?"

Monty took out a yellow legal pad and uncapped his pen. "You're going to tell me. Tell me everything."

"There's nothing to tell."

"Adam, if there were nothing to tell, you wouldn't be in jail on murder charges. Now tell me. I want to know who you were fucking, who you weren't fucking, who is Violet Perkins, and what she could know about you that's got the prosecution so goddamn happy. I want to know what happened the last time you saw Rachel alive, why you left her alone with Albert knowing full well his history of violence. I want to know why there wasn't a single drop of blood on Albert when there was bloodspray on the walls and ceiling. But the first thing I want you to tell me is, did you kill her?"

"This is insanity."

"Be that as it may, I have to ask you. I have to know, Adam. Did you kill her?"

"No. I loved Rachel."

THIRTY-FOUR

He was feeling like a million bucks. No, make that two million. And, surprisingly, Leo found, he wasn't even worried about the phone ringing. He knew it would ring in its own good time. Nothing had gone wrong so far; why would something as little as that all-important phone call disappoint him now? Everything had come together so nicely, so fucking . . . orgasmically, that Leo could hardly believe it was actually happening. Yes, the sensation was sexual, it felt so all-consuming. It was what he'd hoped for—absolutely and without a doubt, it was what he had hoped for—but he had never dared dream it would actually happen. Even if he had dared dream it, he would never have dreamed of everything coming together so perfectly, like two bodies coming together for intercourse. Violet, the Watkins couple, everything. Everything had merged just beautifully.

Around him, the office workers busied themselves in their cubicles, but today Leo was unaware of their presence. Today he didn't even notice the four tiny walls closing in on him, the lamination peeling in long spidery strips from his desk, or the pinch of the surplus chair that was too tight for his round bottom. Today was the day everything was going to change.

Leo kicked his feet up on the wobbly desk and reclined back. The desk chair groaned in protest, pinched his ass a little tighter, but he didn't notice. As he reclined, he could feel the fat Dominican cigar in his breast pocket, pressing comfortably against his chest. The potent aroma of it penetrated his suit jacket and assaulted his nose delightfully. It was an expensive indulgence. For celebration. Celebration after the word came down. And there would be cause to celebrate. He knew that. Just as he knew that he deserved whatever praise he received. After all, he had single-handedly put the whole case together. He knew that. Paula knew that. Soon, Bob would know it. Paula was meeting with him now. And Leo knew, he just knew there was no way Bob could say no. How could he? If it weren't for Leo, there wouldn't even be a case.

He patted the cigar in his breast pocket and smiled contentedly.

The phone rang.

* * *

When she heard the knock on her office door, Paula stubbed out her cigarette and hid the ashtray in a desk drawer.

"Open!"

Leo stuck his head in. "You rang?"

"Yeah, come on in. I've got some news."

"What's up?" Leo asked, and the open expectancy of his face sickened her a little, but only a little. It was going to be unpleasant, and Paula really didn't care for unpleasantness. She knew he was expecting to hear good news—all is forgiven, please come home—but, in the words of Theodore Roosevelt, tough titty.

Paula retrieved her ashtray back out of the desk and lit another cigarette. She exhaled a long plume of smoke and said, "Word just came down."

"Yeah?"

"Bob wants me to handle the case myself."

"He does?"

"That's right."

"And second chair?"

Paula took a deep mental breath. "Bob will be second chair."

"What?" The word barely made a sound as it fell from Leo's mouth. To Paula, it sounded like what you might hear come out of the mouth of a man who had just taken a vicious blow to the stomach. Leo took a deep breath. "Why would Bob want second chair? That makes no sense."

"Think about it. It's Monty Lee's brother. This is about

justice, but it's also a little bit about revenge. A way to send Monty Lee a message. Settle accounts."

"I wanted to settle some accounts myself."

"I know. It's your case. You did all the work. You made the case. I told Bob, but he doesn't want you in the courtroom. This shouldn't be a surprise to you. Bob Fox is not a man who forgives and forgets."

"Fuck Bob. This is my case."

"I know. I'm sorry. I was your advocate in there, believe me. I told Bob I wanted you in the courtroom, backing me up, but he wouldn't go for it."

"Did you tell him there would be no case if it weren't for me?"

"Of course I did."

"You guys were gonna file it away. You were just gonna file it away! I made this case! It's mine! How can you?"

"Leo, come on, you're overreacting. You'll get credit."

"Yeah, right! Oh, thanks, Leo, for gathering all the evidence. Thanks, Leo, for finding and interviewing all the witnesses. Thanks, Leo, for telling us there was a fucking murder in the first fucking place!"

"Leo, I'm sorry."

"'Your faithful fucking servant.' Fuck you."

Paula arched a carefully plucked eyebrow at Leo. Pity only went so far, and she sure as hell wasn't going to tolerate his verbal abuse. "I think you're forgetting who's the servant and who's the master." She watched as Leo began to pace in front of her desk. He was growing more and more agitated as the magnitude of just how badly he had been swindled sank in. Paula had expected things to get ugly. She had planned for it. She would let him work himself up, let him vent his righteous anger, but then she would yank the leash. There was only so much shit she was willing to take.

"You don't want to make an enemy of me, too. I told you, I'm sorry. I did everything I could to get you in that courtroom. Don't blame me if you burned your bridges."

Leo ran his hand across his smooth head, his fingers for once not registering the lack of hair. His pant legs flapped as he paced. He was simply not able to comprehend this was happening.

"I just can't believe you guys would pull it out from under me like that."

"I know."

"I feel like I've been sucker punched."

"I know."

"You know! What the fuck do you know? You have no idea!"

His voice boomed out at her, and he slammed his fists violently down on Paula's desk, hard enough to send the ashtray spinning into the air, cigarette butts twisting lazy curlicues over the desktop. Paula jerked back involuntarily. It was a reflex. Just as when a normally docile pet bites its master's hand, she pulled back, stunned. Leo's face had gone a color Paula couldn't quite put a name to, and for the first time ever, she felt afraid of Leo Hewitt. She was afraid he might do something, well, crazy. His rage was absolute. Then she got hold of herself. *Okay, the man's about to go ballistic, but, hey, let's remember, it's only Leo.* Okay, yes, it was only Leo. For a second there, she'd been scared, but that had just been a reflex. Fear was a controllable emotion, and she'd be damned if she'd let him know that he'd caused her to fear him. Never show fear. That was something she'd learned as a little girl growing up around farm animals in rural Georgia. No matter how vicious the animal, you could always keep the upper hand if you showed no fear. If a mongrel dog confronted you, growling and barking, you were dead if you showed fear. What you did was bark back. Louder. You had to go to the dog's level. You had to make yourself mad. And you had to let the animal see your anger. And fuck this little man. Just who the fuck did he think he was yelling at? She wasn't going to sit here and take this shit off the likes of him.

"Leo, you had best get hold of yourself or you'll find yourself back out on the street. And I fucking mean it! You will show me the respect I've earned! I do not have to, and I will not tolerate your belligerent attitude. I told you that I did everything I could for you. End of discussion. Now get the hell out of my office." Her words were harsh, and she liked the sound of them. They had the impact she intended. Just as a loud noise scares a barking dog, Leo heeled.

"I'm sorry, Paula. Oh Jesus, I'm sorry. I'm not trying to take it out on you. I know you did everything you could. I mean, we're friends, right? It's not your fault. I'm sorry. It's just that . . . This was my case. You know? This was gonna be my—"

"I know," she said, and inwardly smiled.

PART THREE

There's men that somehow just grip your eyes,
and hold them hard like a spell;
And such was he, and he looked to me
like a man who had lived in hell . . .
The music almost died away . . . then it burst
like a pent-up flood;
And it seemed to say, "Repay, repay,"
and my eyes were blind with blood.
The thought came back of an ancient wrong,
and it stung like a frozen lash,
And the lust awoke to kill, to kill . . .
then the music stopped with a crash . . .

—ROBERT W. SERVICE,

"THE SHOOTING OF DAN McGREW"

THIRTY-FIVE

It is very cold in this cell. But not dark. The lights stay on all day and all night, stark, fluorescent, and humming. But still, the darkness is with me here. Inside me. It has not left. If you are unlucky enough to have known the dark as a young man, then wherever you go for the rest of your life, it stays with you, for darkness is a movable feast.

Paradoxically, I find that I don't mind the dark. Other things bother me. There are so many things ahead of me, I can hardly wait for them to arrive. I see now that my journey into the light has only just begun. Eugene O'Neill called his autobiographical play *Long Day's Journey into Night*. Mine will be the inverse.

Monty tells me that my predicament is the topic du jour. I read the papers and see an out-of-date photograph of myself on the television news. So be it. I know that I will emerge from this unsullied—reborn and new. The process has begun. The stage is set. They have finished with the process of voir dire, jury selection. Monty tells me *voir dire* is a French expression. It means "to speak the truth." We shall see, we shall see.

I believe that I am running a fever. My head is hot and my body aches. Dreams stalk my nights. In the mornings, I awake shivering, my thin mattress soaked through with foul-smelling night sweat. And what is worse, I remember the dreams.

They were saying that I deliberately used Albert to kill Rachel. That I used Albert as an instrument of death. That is what they were saying. Now they say I killed her with my own hands. They don't know yet that Rachel was dead to me for years before she died. And Albert, Albert is my son. He is also Rachel's son. He is a merging of the two of us. The sum of the parts that does not equal the whole.

I feel the fever on me again; my thoughts grow unclear, confused.

THIRTY-SIX

"And we will also show that Mr. Adam Lee not only premeditated his wife's murder, but bragged about it before the body was even cold."

Paula loved this part. Like Leo, she loved all of it, but the opening was her favorite. It must be how an actor felt. If it was, she could certainly see the allure of stardom. Because right now, she was a star. The jury her audience. And they hung on her every word. Her every mannerism. It was tougher for a woman, but that made it just that much more exciting. A female trial lawyer walked a very fine line indeed. Any excess in any direction could be lethal. It could alienate jurors. If you came across as too confident, you might piss off the older gentleman who believes women should know their place. Too demure and you risked appearing weak in your convictions. A dress too short, you looked like a flirt. A dress too long, you looked like a spinster prude. Wear a business suit and half of them would label you a lesbian. A male trial lawyer, as long as he didn't have obvious personality flaws, could pretty much just make sure his tie matched his shirt and go to town (and even if his tie didn't match, there would be a woman on the jury who felt sorry for him and wanted to take care of him). But Paula had it all together. Every aspect of her image was presented in just the right doses.

Image was the most valuable lesson she had learned from her mentor, Judge Elizabeth Duran. Elizabeth Duran, who had eventually presided over the Guaraldi case, had been among the first female judges elected to the Superior Court bench in Fulton County and was a figure of aspiration for many young female lawyers. When Paula had still been a student in law school, she had applied for and gotten a coveted clerking job in Judge Duran's office. The two clicked right away. Duran had taken an immediate liking to Paula, and at the time Paula supposed she must have reminded Duran of herself when she was younger. Even then, Paula possessed the steadfast tenacity, the near-Machiavellian determination that would be the hallmark of her legal career. Because of this and the fact that Paula was putting herself through school on a budget of poverty, Duran took Paula under her wing. She tutored Paula on the finer points of the law and courtroom politics. The woman had nothing but disdain for the people who plied the laws, but the law itself she loved. In fact, the law seemed to be her only love. She had no social or romantic contacts to Paula's knowledge. In private, Elizabeth Duran was a salty woman, a heavy drinker not given to niceties or small talk. If she was not discussing law or some aspect of law, she simply had nothing to say.

Paula remembered an afternoon of instruction in Duran's office. Duran paced the highly polished hardwood floors in her stocking feet, a tumbler of scotch in one hand, a cigarette smoldering away in the other. She had been talking at length of the fine line a woman must navigate to become a successful trial lawyer. She had come to the topic of cosmetics, and although she wore not even a hint of makeup herself, claiming a judge could look any way she damn well pleased, she instructed Paula on the finer points of cosmetology. (At fifty-seven, Duran's angular features could have done with a few softening strokes of the makeup brush, but Paula wouldn't have dared to presume to say so.) "You have to wear it," Duran had said in her gravelly voice, sipping her scotch. "Even if you don't need it, you have to wear it. Just so you don't come across like a militant bull dyke. But it has to be understated. Too much, and you're going to walk into that courtroom looking like a hooker in search of a twenty-dollar blowjob." Over the years, Paula had found that all of Duran's wisdom had proven to be true. Regardless of how the relationship had ended, Duran had taught her a lot.

Around the time Paula was ready to give up her clerking job for a position in the DA's office, Duran had invited her for a weekend at her beach house on Jekyll Island. On the second night there, Duran had made a blatant, drunken pass at Paula. Paula demurred at the offer in an offhand way. Thanks, but no thanks. But Duran had insisted, claimed that Paula "owed" her something for all that she had done for her. The situation escalated into an ugly confrontation and ended with Paula driving five dark hours back to the city. They had seen each other in court several times over the years, but neither ever acknowledged what was between them.

And Paula thought of Elizabeth Duran now as she looked each of the jurors in the eye, knowing exactly how each of them perceived her. And she knew that they couldn't help but be impressed with her. Impressed with her smart good looks and unassuming authority. There was a hardness inside her, a ruthlessness she was proud of, but that was hidden away now. They saw only what she wanted them to see. And, best of all, she was on. Everything was clicking. If she was on during the opening, it set a winning pace for her side for the whole trial. And now her favorite part was coming up. The part where you have to point. It was standard practice, but she got a secret thrill from it. If you were clicking the way you thought you were, you could win jurors over to your side before even a single piece of evidence had been presented. Just with that finger held out in accusation.

She let her eyes meet each of the jurors'. Let each of them know she was talking directly to them and was hiding nothing. Then she turned from the jury and pointed.

"Yes, this man. This man right here. Murdered his wife. His wife of twenty-one years. And tried to place the blame for the murder on his mentally retarded son."

And she turned back to the jury. More eye contact. A dramatic pause. *Let the accusation sink in. Take them back into your confidence. Wrap it up.*

"And they're going to try again. To place the blame. On a defenseless, mentally disabled man. The defendant's own son. I'm not here today to place blame. I'm here to place the facts. The evidence. In front of you. So you can decide for yourselves. Don't be afraid to make the right decision. Thank you."

Paula took her seat next to Bob at the prosecution table. He smiled at her, partly because he was impressed with her performance, partly so the jury could see his confidence in her.

Judge Kenneth Cray, a small, wiry man of sixty, nodded to Monty and motioned for him to proceed with his opening statement. Monty clapped his briefcase shut, thus commanding the jury's attention and communicating his irritation with the prosecution's outlandish accusations.

"She's right," he said, at once acknowledging Paula's words while delegating her to nothing more than a *she*. Not *Ms. Manning*, not *my colleague*, not *the prosecution*, but nothing more than an anonymous *she*. Monty, too, reveled in the intricacies of courtroom theater. He relished the subtle psychological war that the lawyers waged, each side meticulously manipulating every facet of what the jury would see and hear in the hopes of gaining a minute psychological edge. He knew that with his good looks alone, the minute he stepped into any courtroom he was already one step ahead of the competition. Since he had been a boy, he was well aware of the fact that his appearance just made people like him, and he used that knowledge to his benefit. People were just drawn to him. It made his everyday life more pleasant, and it was his greatest weapon in the courtroom. He knew that his fine features caused people to want to be in his favor. They wanted him to like them, men and women alike. And it was easy, so easy to parlay this need of theirs to be in his good grace into a winning judgment. It was just a question of making the other side look bad.

"She's right. There is no blame." Paula never actually said there was no blame, but it was close enough to what she had said that the jurors now believed she had. "How can you blame a mentally handicapped man who has no awareness of his own actions?"

Now he stood and faced the jury. "You can't. But the prosecution wants to blame someone. Who? Mr. Adam Lee, whose only crime was to bring home his son to visit his mother. His son's mother, who was so depressed and sick that she couldn't even leave her own house to visit her only son. So Mr. Lee brought his son home from the hospital to see his mother. A tragic accident occurred, yes. And Mr. Lee will probably blame himself forever. As we all blame ourselves for mistakes we couldn't have foreseen."

From the spectators' gallery, Leo's glum moon face caught Monty's eye, but he quickly looked away from him. He let his eyes meet each of the jurors'.

"Is Adam Lee a perfect husband? No. Is Adam Lee a perfect father? No. Does that make Adam Lee guilty of murder? Again, no."

Now, just as important as Paula's finger-pointing, Monty walked over to Adam. He stood behind his brother. He knew that you had to get the jury to look at your client. Let them begin to be comfortable with him. Let them become familiar with him. Later on, they would find it more difficult to convict if it came to that. He had already coached Adam on eye contact. You've got to look them in the eye. You don't stare, don't make them uncomfortable. Just let them know that you have nothing to hide.

"You may have heard that Adam is my brother. It's true. I'm here today not because Adam is my brother, but because I know Adam is innocent. Don't let the prosecution make you think otherwise, because they will try. Have you ever heard of mudslinging? That's what's going to happen during the course of this trial. The prosecution is going to sling some mud."

Monty placed his hands on Adam's shoulders. You touch your client. Always. Let them know you genuinely like him, genuinely feel he's innocent.

"They're going to try to make Adam Lee look like a bad person. Well, guess what? Adam had an affair during the course of his marriage. He's not proud of it; in fact, he's ashamed of it. You can be a bad person. You can be a good person. It doesn't matter. If you're innocent, you're innocent. And Adam Lee is innocent."

THIRTY-SEVEN

"YOU CAN BE A BAD PERSON"
Attorneys Set Strategies in Lee Trial

by Anne Hunter

staff writer

During today's opening statements of the Lee trial, attorney Monty Lee, defending his brother, Adam Lee, characterized his brother's extramarital affairs by stating that "you can be a bad person" and still be innocent. Adam Lee stands accused of murdering his wife, Rachel Lee, last October.

For the prosecution, Assistant District Attorney Paula Manning accused Adam Lee of trying to frame his developmentally disabled son, Albert, for his wife's murder.

Ms. Manning also stated that the prosecution will show that Adam Lee bragged about murdering his wife "before the body was even cold."

The district attorney's office continues to deny rumors of former assistant district attorney Leo Hewitt's involvement in this trial. One insider claimed that District Attorney Bob Fox "wouldn't let Leo Hewitt investigate a cat up a tree," in reference to Mr. Hewitt's mishandling of key evidence during the trial of child killer Frank Guaraldi.

The prosecution is expected to begin calling witnesses Monday.

THIRTY-EIGHT

"Yes, we were waiting in line together. Herbert, that's my husband, he offered the girl his coat."

"By 'the girl' you're referring to Mr. Lee's companion, Constance Perkins?"

"That's right."

"And did you talk with Mr. Lee?"

"Oh yes. Yes we did."

"Does anything from that conversation stick out in your memory?"

"It certainly does. That man said—"

"You mean Adam Lee?"

"Yes. That man. He said he was a widower."

Leo felt sick to his stomach. It was making him sick to see Paula getting all the credit for his hard work. This was turning into the kind of trial that makes careers. All the leg-work and tenacity that went behind a slick-as-shit set-'em-up and mow-'em-down murder trial was paying off beautifully. Paula would be remembered for this one, and he would be forgotten. All the hard work and sheer bloody luck that had gone into finding just this one witness would be credited to Paula. No one would ever know how he'd kept pushing to find Violet Perkins when Paula was ready to write the whole thing off. No one would ever know how he kept pushing Violet to tell her story over and over and over again, making sure he had every last detail of that weekend. How he had pushed her until she remembered the nice old man who'd lent her his jacket. Pushed until she remembered that Adam had told the man's wife that Rachel was dead. Which was great, except there was no way to trace a couple of retirees from a chance encounter at a roadside tourist trap. And no one would ever know how Leo had been ready to accept the fact that he would never be able to find this old couple, that even if he had the resources, it would most likely prove impossible. Except for one thing. Except for the fact that he had, for no real reason, asked Violet whatever happened to the jacket. "It's hanging up in my closet," she said. And so it was. A Georgia Bulldogs team jacket. A nice one. The old man was going to be sorry he'd lost it, but he had a smart wife, so getting it back to him wouldn't be a problem. The wife had sewn the old man's name and address inside the collar.

"And this was in?"

"October. October second. I remember because it was two days after mine and Herbert's anniversary."

"What time?"

"About noon. Right around lunchtime."

"At noon on October second, six and a half hours before Rachel Lee's body was discovered, Adam Lee informed you his wife was dead?"

"Yes."

"Anything else you remember from that conversation?"

"Oh, yes. I'll never forget it. He said he was glad she was dead. That she was a . . . a . . . a bitch."

Leo couldn't help but smile. It was sheer perfection. Paula was even using his prepared, numbered questions. The questions themselves weren't the important thing, it was the order in which they were asked. So that the last thing the jury would hear was Adam Lee calling his dead wife a bitch.

He watched Monty push back from his chair and approach Mrs. Herbert Watkins, and smiled again. Leo knew exactly what he would ask the woman if he were Monty, and he had coached her accordingly. Mrs. Watkins was a tough old bird; he doubted Monty would be able to ruffle her feathers.

"Mrs. Watkins, I just want to ask you few questions. Now, you say that my client, Adam Lee, said to you that he was a widower. Did you get the feeling that he might be putting you on, having a little fun at your expense?"

"He was serious. Dead serious."

"October second, that was five months ago. Is there any

chance your memory of the incident has faded in those five months?"

"All memories fade with time, Mr. Lee, but this particular memory remains fresh in my mind, because, as I said, it was so close to our anniversary and that man was so rude to me."

"Yes, all memories do fade over time. And what you perceived as rudeness could have been a slight joke at your expense."

Paula stood and said, "Objection. Is that a question or a statement?"

"Sustained. Please rephrase as a question, Mr. Lee."

"Withdrawn."

Leo watched as Monty nodded deferentially to Judge Cray. He watched Monty turn to sit back down, and then change his mind and turn back to Mrs. Watkins. *Don't do it,* Leo thought. *Don't do it. Just accept the fact that you've been burned. Badly. By a seventy-year-old woman. Just dismiss the witness and sit back down. Take your lumps.*

"Are you a drinker, Mrs. Watkins?"

Oh Christ, not that old chestnut. He was desperate. Almost didn't coach her against that one, didn't think the guy would be stupid enough to try it.

"Certainly not."

"So you had nothing to drink that day?"

Leo saw Paula stand to object, as she rightly should. The question had been asked and answered. But Mrs. Herbert Watkins beat Paula to the punch. She turned to the judge and said, "Your Honor, I object." The entire courtroom erupted with laughter. The jury, the spectators, the press, even Judge Cray hung his head and covered his face. Anne Hunter would use it in her next day's headline. Monty walked back to his seat, ridiculed.

And Leo watched it all. Days unwound and he watched the parade of witnesses and evidence, watched the drama unfold and saw the prosecution begin to wrap up its case against Adam Lee. He watched the case he had meticulously put together as it came to its beautiful fruition. He took some bitter satisfaction in knowing he was still a damn good trial lawyer, even if he wasn't the one getting the glory. And he watched it all play out in front of him, and he took bitter, bitter satisfaction.

"Your Honor, the prosecution would like to call its last witness. Constance Perkins."

The courtroom grew quiet as Violet headed for the stand. This was the witness everybody had been waiting for. The other woman. In her strut to the front of the courtroom, Violet's body language proclaimed to any and all that she was finally, ultimately justified. The world could now acknowledge her role in all of this. She wanted to be acknowledged for what she was. The other woman. The bailiff swore her in, and Leo noted that she was wearing a provocatively short-hemmed skirt despite his strenuous urging that she dress conservatively. It was a small thing, but it was bothersome. So far, it was the one thing that hadn't gone exactly as planned.

Leo saw a male juror crane his head in a less-than-discreet attempt at catching a flash of thigh. When Leo had interviewed her, she had grown more and more excited at the prospect of her part in the trial. She used terms like *a kept woman, mistress,* and *key witness* when referring to herself in conversation.

Paula approached her key witness, and Leo noted that even from as far back as he was, Violet's lipstick was alarmingly red. He began to wish for a cigar.

"Would you state your name for the record, please."

"Constance Perkins. But you can call me Violet."

Leo groaned. The beginning of their case had gone better than it probably should have. It looked like they were going to pay for that good luck now. Paula stuck to the questions Leo had prepared, and Violet responded more or less as he had coached her. There were some deviations, a few overly cute asides, but no real harm done. Mostly it was a lot of leg crossing and cleavage thrusting and generally acting like a tart that was blowing her credibility all to hell.

"And what was his response?"

"That he wished his wife would die."

"Adam Lee said that he wished his wife, Rachel Lee, were dead?"

"Yes. He said that Rachel would be better off dead."

"Thank you, Ms. Perkins."

Leo sighed. Not a bad finish. Not bad at all. Considering. Then Monty stood up. Then everything went to hell.

"Ms. Perkins, good afternoon. You go by Violet, is that right?"

"Yes.

"May I call you that?"

Violet smiled at Monty like she was sitting at a bar in a nightclub and he had just bought her a fuzzy navel. She cooed, "I'd like that."

"Violet. That's an unusual name. Pretty."

Leo watched as Paula finally stood to address what was starting to sound like dialogue out of a porno film. "The originality of the witness's name is without relevance."

Judge Cray waved his finger at Monty. "This isn't social hour, Mr. Lee."

"Well, let me get to the point then. Violet, do you make a habit of seducing married men?"

Paula jumped up and said, "Objection. Argumentative."

"Just trying to establish the character of the witness, Your Honor."

"Overruled. Play nice, Mr. Lee. And you may address the witness as Ms. Perkins."

"Well, Ms. Perkins? Do you often have affairs with married men?"

"No, I don't." Violet's face had taken a pouty turn; her lower lip protruded, full and red.

"But you did know, didn't you? That Adam Lee was married?"

"Yes, I was aware."

"Yet you still chose to accompany him on this romantic weekend getaway?"

"I wasn't the one cheating, he was."

"Well, it takes two to tango, doesn't it?"

Monty earned a spattering of laughter with this last remark. He had stolen it from a movie he saw on cable television the night before. Feeling somewhat uplifted, he grew bolder.

"Were you angry, Violet, uh, Ms. Perkins, when Mr. Lee didn't call you after your tryst?"

"Objection. No foundation," Paula said.

"Withdrawn. Did Mr. Lee call you after your weekend together?"

"No, I'd changed my—"

"Yes or no will do."

"No. He didn't."

"I see."

"No, you don't see. I changed my number so he couldn't call me. I didn't want—"

"Your Honor, I ask that those last remarks be stricken from the record and the witness be instructed to answer only the questions asked of her."

"So stricken. The jury will disregard those last remarks. Ms. Perkins, you are not here to volunteer information."

Monty walked nonchalantly to the defense table, pretended to straighten some papers, and turned back to Violet. "Ms. Perkins, one final thing."

Here we go, Leo thought. The one final thing. The one final thing is seldom final and is always, without exception, something that will come as a total surprise to the other side. What will it be? Satanism? Drug dependency? Something fun, no doubt. The one final thing is always fun.

"How did you meet Adam Lee?"

"At work. I was temping at the hospital where his son stays."

"Yes, but what exactly were you doing the very first time you met Mr. Lee?"

Paula objected, mostly because she had no idea where this was going. "How many times must the witness answer the same question?"

Monty turned to Judge Cray. "Your Honor, I simply want the witness to tell the court exactly what task she was performing when she first met the defendant."

"Overruled. The witness may answer the question."

"I told you, I was working," Violet said. Her bottom lip pouted out again, but not quite as red now. Those pouts had worn off a lot of lipstick.

"Come on, Ms. Perkins, you know what I'm driving at, don't you?" Monty asked.

"I'm sure I don't."

"Isn't it true, Ms. Perkins, that you were masturbating Mr. Lee's son?"

Paula jumped to her feet and barely kept her voice below a yell. "Your Honor, this is outrageous."

"The facts are the facts, Your Honor," Monty said. "I can't help it if Ms. Manning finds the facts uncomfortable. This relates directly to character."

"Overruled. Answer the question, Ms. Perkins."

Violet's mouth was set like a little girl facing down a spoonful of castor oil. "I do it to help them sleep."

"Do what?" Monty asked.

"I—"

"Did Adam Lee catch you masturbating his son, Albert?"

"Yes."

"Thank you. I have nothing further."

No way was Paula going to let it end on this note. She approached the witness box.

"Redirect, Your Honor?"

"Go ahead."

"Ms. Perkins, when Mr. Lee asked you if Adam Lee called you after your weekend together, you said no, but you wanted to explain why."

"Your Honor," Monty asked, "unless Ms. Perkins is a mind reader, how could she possibly know why my client did not call her?"

"Sustained."

Paula continued. "Okay, Ms. Perkins, is there any fact, within your scope of knowledge, that would have prevented Adam Lee from being able to contact you by telephone?"

"Yes. I had my number changed to an unlisted one."

"And you didn't give Adam Lee your new phone number?"

"No."

"Why?"

"Because I didn't want to hear from him ever again."

"Why not?"

"Adam is a very sick person."

Monty objected. "Is Ms. Perkins seriously testifying as to my client's state of health?"

Paula pushed ahead. "What do you mean when you say that Adam Lee is a very sick person?"

"He hurt me."

"How exactly did Adam Lee hurt you? Do you mean physically?"

"Physically. Yes. He tied me to the bed and hurt me physically."

"When was this?" Paula asked.

"Our last night in the mountains."

"And how exactly did Adam Lee hurt you physically?"

"He tied me to the bed."

Monty spoke up. "Your Honor, I'm afraid I can't quite see how inventorying the consensual sex acts of Ms. Perkins and Adam Lee is relevant to the case at hand."

"Mr. Lee opened the door to sex acts as an indicator of character," Paula pointed out to the judge.

"You did do that, Mr. Lee. You can't have it both ways. Overruled."

Monty sat down and dared a quick glance at Adam. Adam looked only at the table in front of him.

Paula asked, "Did you agree to let the defendant tie you to the bed?"

"Yes, but I thought it was just going to be for fun. Once he had me tied up, he hurt me."

"What exactly did he do to you once he had you bound?"

"He cut me in tiny places with a knife. He spit on me. When I said no, he raped me, anally. I bled for days. But before he let me go, he used the bathroom on me."

"How do you mean?"

"He peed on me."

"After sodomizing you and lacerating you with a knife blade, Adam Lee degraded you by spitting on you and urinating on you while you were defenseless."

"That's right."

"Why didn't you report this to the police?"

"Because I knew I couldn't prove it. We had been having sex together for a long time. I could hardly believe it myself. I thought I knew Adam. I didn't know he was capable of . . . I just didn't know he was capable."

THIRTY-NINE

I wait for Monty in the interview room. Today, like every other day, the trial did not go well for us. Monty made small victories, but they were Pyrrhic. We lost more ground than we gained. There is much criticism in the press. Criticism of my brother's handling of my case. They say it is a weak defense he has mounted on my behalf. I read with interest the coverage of Anne Hunter. She has been particularly unmerciful in her writings of every aspect of the trial. In the paper today, the Hunter woman continues her tirade. She slants her story toward the "weird sex acts" that transpired between me and Violet, and the "buried rage" that drove me to torture and degradation. She is, of course, quite right in her assessment. She criticizes Monty for not prefiguring the disastrous consequences of a line of questioning that opens the door to sexual histories. Again, she is correct in her assessment. Monty is performing poorly. There is, however, a certain line in her article that reverberates in my mind. A legal analyst, when referring to Monty's ineptitude, says, "it is almost as if he wants his brother to be caught." The words echo in my mind, picking up speed, and I find myself thinking of a time when we were boys. Of a girl I cared for. Of sexual awakenings. Of sexual cruelties.

Monty enters the interview cell, his face a mask of despondency. He has not contacted me since our last disastrous day in court. I wait for him to speak.

"Well, I won't lie to you. I mean, we blew the Perkins woman's credibility all to hell. Made her look like the slut she is. But what was that shit about you tying her up and peeing on her?"

"It was lies."

"Well, it sounded like lies. I hope it sounded like lies to the jury. Like she was desperate to make you look bad. But that old woman hurt us. Hurt us bad. Jesus, did you really say that? That Rachel was dead?"

"I wasn't myself. It was a joke. I didn't mean it."

"Believe me, you don't come across as the joking type. That old woman is going to sink us. How the fuck did they find that old bat? Jesus, I should never have called that bastard Leo."

"No, I would say that was a mistake. One of several." This is the first time I have commented on his performance in a negative light. Indeed, it is the first time I have ever dared criticize my brother.

"What are you trying to say? If you're trying to say something, just fucking say it."

"I'm trying to say that several mistakes have been made."

"Yeah, taking some tramp for a weekend of S&M and water sports, that was a mistake. Running around to the geriatric twins and bragging about how your wife was dead and it didn't really matter because she was a real bitch anyway, that was a mistake. Thinking a jury is gonna believe you if you get on the stand and tell them how you cleaned every microdrop of blood off Albert and washed all of his clothes before the police got to the crime scene, that was a mistake. And you know what else was a mistake, Adam? Killing your wife, that was a mistake."

"It sounds like I need a new lawyer. No wonder you can't convince anybody I'm innocent; you don't believe it yourself."

"What do you expect, Adam? You sure as hell *look* guilty."

"I expect my lawyer to make me look *not* guilty."

"Okay, okay. I'm sorry. It's just that the case is going so badly. I guess I'd rather believe you're guilty than believe I might lose the case. That you might go to prison. Or worse. Because of me. Because I failed."

The moment has passed. Neither of us likes this sort of tension. We assume our old roles of weak and strong. "I have faith in you," I tell him. "It will be because of you that I am set free."

"I pray you're right." He prepares to leave. He has had enough of me for one day. I sicken him. I represent his own failure. "Look, I've got to get to the office. I'm supposed to meet with your shrink, what's his name, Doctor—?"

"Salinger."

"He says he'll tell the jury you're not crazy and he doesn't believe, based on his professional opinion, that you're capable of premeditated murder."

"Premeditated?"

"Well, that's what you're accused of, and Salinger won't testify without the qualification. He says we're all capable of murder given the right amount of rage and provocation."

"You don't think that it will make me look bad, the fact that I've consulted a psychiatrist?"

"Believe me, at this point, it's the last of our worries. He'll also say that your having the affair was a way for you to work through your marriage difficulties, and I'm pretty sure that we can get him to say that what you said to Mrs. Oldster was just a way of letting off steam or some such bullshit. Don't worry. I'm thinking ahead. All is not lost. I still have hope."

Monty clasps my shoulders and gives me a halfhearted hug. I know that in his eyes, I am already lost.

"Anyway, I'll try to come back tonight."

He opens his briefcase and takes out a pair of sunglasses. He puts them on and I remember. I remember the last time I saw those glasses. He was passing me in his car, on my driveway, and the light reflected off them so that his eyes were like two holes of white light. I remember. I—

"What is it?"

"What were you doing at my house that day?"

"What? What day?"

"I passed you in the drive. The weekend Rachel died."

"Oh. She called me over. You know. She was half crazy. Drinking. The pills. I'm sorry, but you know how she was."

"And what exactly did she call you over for?"

"You know."

"No, I don't."

"About how you wanted me to be Albert's godfather. I dropped off the papers. You remember, the ones I refused to sign. Because I was afraid you were planning to do something crazy. Afraid you were up to something bad. And here we are."

"You weren't sleeping with my wife, were you, Monty? My crazy rich wife?"

"You're talking out of your head. You know, of all people, you know how Rachel was. An affair? Come on, Adam. You're under a lot of strain. Are you trying to say that I had something to do with Rachel's death? Adam, you know who killed her. You cleaned the blood off your son, remember?"

"Yes, I remember. I'm just trying to get things straight in my mind."

"Look, just try to get some rest. I was going to tell you later, but I think we'll have to put you on the stand. It's always a big risk, but with everything that's happened, they're going to have to hear it from you. They're going to have to hear you say that you didn't kill her."

"Yes. They will have to hear me say that. I want something from you. I want you to call Anne Hunter. I want to talk to her. I want to tell her my story."

"That's a bad idea."

"I want to do it."

"It's a very bad idea. These people in the press, they twist things around. They're worse than lawyers. You'll regret it."

"Call her for me. It's what I want."

Finally, he agrees. His agreement tells me more than anything else that he believes all is lost. What is one more mistake in an endless series of mistakes? I nod to him as he leaves, and I think of those glasses, the circles of light, like twin summer suns. I think about that summer at the lake when we were boys and the girl we knew. I think about what happened that summer and wonder how it shaped me. I think about that summer and I wonder what my brother, my handsome, handsome brother is capable of.

FORTY

It was the last summer before our parents would die in an automobile accident, but already Monty was the focus of my life. As only a young boy can know, my love and admiration for my older brother was without bounds. He could do no wrong. His every action was, in my eyes at least, flawless. When he threw a baseball, his aim was superb and sure, the pitch almost balletic. And to be the lucky recipient in a game of catch was a privilege without peer. For him to allow me a small portion of his time that might have been more profitably spent with the older boys and their secret society was a magnanimous gesture. Whatever he touched, turned to gold. Indeed, he himself was golden. I followed him constantly, never more than a few steps behind. I had to see all that he did, witness all that he would become, all that he would allow me to become. And, in my most delightful memories, share with him the experiences of boyhood. He taught me how to smoke pilfered cigarettes, how to inhale the smoke that would cause my head to spin and my stomach to roll uneasily. He taught me how to bait a fishing hook with the eye of the minnow impaled through the hook's sharp point. He taught me how to tie a length of thread onto the leg of a June bug and hold on giggling as it flew crazily around our heads. He taught me how to whistle, to swim, to spit, to live. And he taught me other things as well. He taught me degradation, cruelty, and spite.

That summer, the last summer our parents would ever see before their lives were snuffed out in a heap of twisted metal, I was ten, Monty fourteen. Our family was vacationing at Lake Armistead in the North Carolina mountains. There was a girl. Twelve, possibly thirteen years old. Her family rented another cabin on the lake in the summers, and, over the years, our families grew close, socialized. Her parents and ours would sit out on the covered porch and play card games long into the mountain nights. From the yard we could see their cigarettes spinning orange phantom trails in the summer dark, glow and wink out as if with some secret rhythm like fireflies mating. There were cold gin drinks and much slapping of mosquitoes and, as the hour grew late, drunken laughter. Our mother would sleep past noon after one of these nights and not fully recover until well into the next evening. The next card game, the next drink.

The girl wore braces on her legs. Cumbersome metal

braces to straighten out recalcitrant legs from curving inward by God knows what childhood disease. We made fun of
her. Or, rather, Monty made fun of her and I joined in, already a firm believer of my brother as hero. In my eyes, he
could do no wrong. And if the teasing should go a little too
far, should it border on cruelty of an adult nature, then so be
it. My brother knew what he was doing. If jamming lighted
matches into the crevices of her metal braces was what Monty
said was the thing to do, then I did it. If deliberately tripping
her so that we might make fun as she struggled to get back
up was Monty's idea of idle diversion, then that was what we
did. Monty always knew the correct action to take. I had to
believe that. I had to believe it then, because doubt was sac-
rilege. How could you doubt what you aspired to become? I
had no choice but to believe it later. Later, when adolescence
should have brought a sense of independence and questioning, Monty had assumed the roles of mother, father, and con-
fessor. But for that summer, we were just boys, growing strong
and lean and tan in the mountain sun.

Despite our never-ending teasing, the girl, Denise, never
considered staying away from us. I didn't blame her. I too
would have borne any humiliation rather than be denied my
brother's presence. I suspect that for her as well as me, Monty
was like a magnet. She just wanted to be around him, within
his field of current, even if the price was her dignity. And
Monty was handsome. Already his shoulders were wide and
strong, his legs lean and muscled and dusted with sun-
bleached hair. Puberty had blossomed him into a strikingly

beautiful (there is no other word) young man. And this beauty would eventually deform his mind so that he saw women only as instruments to be used for his own pleasure. Since he could have any girl, and later, any woman he chose, why not have them all? Indeed, if his cruel taunts and constant degradation could not keep Denise from seeking out his male beauty, how must it have affected his emerging ego?

There was an incident. Our parents and Denise's parents had gone down the mountain and into the small town for an afternoon of shopping. Monty, as the oldest, was given charge of Denise and me. We were to stay with Denise at her parents' cabin. Our mother had given Monty and me a solemn look and told us to behave ourselves. Denise's mother did likewise and cautioned Denise to stay away from the lake. No sooner had our parents' car left than Monty started in on Denise.

"Hey, Denise, wanna go swimmin'? Oh, wait, that's right, you can't swim, you're a fuckin' cripple."

She took it like always, outwardly annoyed, but inwardly, I knew, simply glad to have some degree of Monty's attention.

"Sticks and stones, Monty Lee. Why can't you just be nice for once?"

"I don't wanna be nice. I like bein' mean." Then he added, "Especially bein' mean to cripples like you." He must have had some sense of his power over her.

"Oh, you're mean all right. You should try to be more like Adam."

"You're crazy and a cripple," I said, wanting to demonstrate quite clearly that I was on Monty's side in this and all matters. Still, I disliked talking harshly to her. Not that I was above such things as talking harshly to girls; far from it, I reveled in it on the school playground. And it was not a sense of pity for her, of that I'm sure. In truth, Denise was actually an attractive girl. Her hair was jet black and constantly clean and shiny. I sometimes daydreamed of touching it or smelling it. In her hair was hidden a lovely paradox that I thought only I could see. Her hair was so black that sometimes, in the sun's light, the faint curls managed to somehow capture the light and refract it back in secret rainbows of color. I sometimes wondered what it might be like to kiss her. These thoughts would set off a buzzing in my head and cloud my mind for hours, wonderful hours. I of course would never admit to these feelings, because Denise was clearly a person to be scorned, beneath even my idle daydreams. Monty had unequivocally demonstrated that, had rigidly set the parameters that I must follow. She was not worthy of admiration in even an innocent boyhood crush. Yet, for all of that, could a boy be blamed for noting with delight that her breasts were just developing? Could I be blamed for thinking of the small swells beneath her cotton shirts? Thinking of these things late into the night and coveting a secret erection beneath the blankets. Can a boy be blamed for his awakening sexuality?

"You better be nice to me."

"Or what?"

"Or else you'll never find out."

"Find out what?"

"My secret."

"You haven't got a secret," Monty said.

"Wouldn't you like to know."

"What could a freak know that would be worth knowing?"

"Be nice and you'll find out."

"This is as nice as I get. Tell me the secret. I'm gettin' bored."

"It's not a secret you tell. It's a secret thing."

"A secret thing?"

The pleasure in her eyes was unmistakable. She had actually gotten my brother to express interest. "Yeah. I took it from my dad."

"Let's see it."

"Are you gonna be nice?"

"Just get it."

How could she refuse? I could not have. She turned stiffly on her braces and lurched toward her bedroom. From her room, we could hear drawers opening and closing. We heard the sounds of metal fasteners unsprung. "Hurry up already," Monty yelled to her. After a while, she was back. She came through the door wearing a new pair of clingy cotton shorts. The braces were off her legs. There were white cross marks engraved in the flesh of her thighs where the metal braces had pressed against her pale skin. She walked with an alarming grace.

"See, my legs are normal. I'm not a cripple. I just have to wear the braces so my legs won't grow in crooked. I have nice legs. See?"

Monty was having none of it. "Is that your secret? Big fuckin' deal. You'll always be a cripple to me."

"I thought you were gonna be nice. And besides, that's not the secret. This is the secret." And she pulled her hand out from behind her back, and held out a nearly full bottle of gin. "I stole it from my dad. A little at a time in an empty bottle."

"Oh, yeah?" Monty's expression had changed from one of idle contempt to one of outright intrigue. His face clearly stated that this was truly a secret thing. And at that moment, how could Denise feel anything other than triumphant, just as I felt defeat. Something passed between them in that brief moment, and it sickened me.

"Let's get drunk," she said.

Monty arched his eyebrows in doubt. It was a mannerism he would use repeatedly as an adult in the courtroom to communicate his disdain silently and effectively. "You'll get sick. You can't drink liquor."

"Sure I can," Denise said, and turned the bottle up. She took a large gulp. A shudder ran through her body as the gin settled in her stomach. She wiped her mouth with the back of her hand and held the bottle out to Monty. I have no idea if he had ever drunk before or even wanted to, but he had no choice now. It was drink or look weak in the eyes of the outcast. He took a drink, tentative at first, but it quickly grew into a gulp. His swallow would be larger than hers had been, of that there would be no question should such issues be brought into discussion later. He winced at the bite of the alcohol but didn't cough or choke. That would have been unthinkable, humiliating. He handed the bottle back to her, and she offered it to me. Monty waved her hand away.

"No. Not Adam. He's too young."

I protested, but only halfheartedly, partly because Monty had spoken and I could never break his resolve, but mostly because I wanted nothing to do with this. At the same time, I also hated the fact that they were sharing a secret without me. Now I was the weaker. The uninitiated. How proud she must feel, having insinuated herself between us, having gotten through to Monty, being allowed to bask in his glow, exist within his magnetic field.

Denise took another swallow and passed the bottle back to Monty. They drank in a solemn silence like cultists administering a lethal poison. At other times they would both erupt in gales of laughter without a word having been exchanged, as though a joke had passed between them by telepathy. They drank until there was only a few inches of liquid left in the bottle. When Monty reached again for the gin, she held it away from him.

"No, it's not free anymore," she said, and giggled.

"Whadda ya mean, not free?" Monty's speech was slurred, and it scared me. The liquor had changed him. I believed that then, that it was the alcohol at fault. Later, I would believe that the liquor had not so much changed him as intensified him. Given us a glimpse of the Monty to come.

"I mean you have to pay for it," Denise said.

"Pay for it? How much?"

"Not money."

"What?"

"A dare."

"Fine."

"You have to touch my leg. To prove it's normal."

"You're fuckin' crazy. I'm not touchin' your fucked-up leg."

"Okay. I guess you don't want a drink then."

Monty thought it over. As he thought, his upper body weaved like a bowling pin about to topple over. Then a smile came to his lips. "Okay. I'll touch your leg."

They both grew quiet. Even drunk, they both knew this was a monumental thing. I did too. It seemed as though they had forgotten about my being in the room with them. But I knew Monty had not forgotten me, and even if he had, he had not forgotten himself. This was a trick. I knew it. It had to be. My brother, drunk or not, would never, never ever, give in so easily to such blatant manipulation. He had something planned. He would touch her leg and then fall to the floor in mock agony. He would hold on to his arm and say she had infected it with her disability. He would simply snatch the gin bottle from her hand and laugh at her with contempt.

Monty reached out and tentatively placed his fingertips on her shin. Roughly he cupped his hand around her smooth calf and fumbled his hand under her knee and continued his caress jerkily up the inside her thigh.

"You're right. It's normal."

I waited for the trick, the insult, but I was disappointed.

There was no joke. Worse still, Monty's voice was different. It was thick, husky, and I knew that it was not from the alcohol. And that alarmed me even more. Where was the punch line to this awful, awful joke?

"I told you. It feels good, doesn't it?"

"Yeah, it's okay. Now gimme." Monty took the bottle and drank from it. When he finished, he held the bottle back out to Denise, and when she reached for it, he jerked it back.

"Hey!"

"It's not free anymore."

"Okay. What do you want?"

"I dare you. I dare you to take off your shirt and let me see your tits."

"You'd like that, wouldn't you?"

"As a matter of fact, I would."

Denise needed no time to think it over. This was what she wanted, what she had planned all along, I believed. "Okay, I don't care. I have a good body." She pulled off her top, and then her bra without his asking. Monty reached out and grabbed one of her budding breasts. He held it with a rough awkwardness, kneading it with callous curiosity.

"You see. I have a good body. You wanna see more?" Denise asked.

"Sure."

She pulled off her shorts and her pink panties. I stared, but I didn't see her. I didn't want to see her.

Naked, she turned to Monty. "Now you." And Monty did. He pulled off his shirt, pants, and socks. He stood before her, allowing her to look at his body. His underwear bulged out in front with his excitement. He pulled off the briefs. His penis was engorged and huge. It seemed an enraged exclamation, an appendage of anger. The thick swatch of pubic hair that engulfed it alarmed me. A dense, profuse tangle that stood out in coarse contrast to his other, sun-bleached hair. It looked obscene.

Her genitals were nearly hairless. Faint dark curls were only beginning to sprout in a discernible triangle shape. The lips of her vagina were smooth and discreet and somehow alien. My head began to hum and buzz, but not in the pleasant fashion of my romantic daydreams, but in an unpleasant, sickening throb. Denise lay on the floor and parted her legs as Monty approached, and I could see the pink flesh inside her. My head ached like a rotten tooth and wanted to crack open with the wasplike hum deafening me from the inside out. And yet, for all that, there was still a perverse excitement, and, I was ashamed to discover, a stiffening in my pants. I watched as my brother took her. The first girl to capture my romantic interest and to stir my burgeoning sexual desire. I watched as my brother took all of that away from me. He was rough, awkward, and there was blood. She bit back her pain and closed her eyes in grim determination. She was going to let this happen, no matter what the cost. She was going to let this golden boy have her. She was going to savor his wanting of her, his clumsy passion for her, yes, this passion directed at her. Tears streamed from her eyes and I could not tell if it was from happiness or pain, but I knew it was one of the two.

She was wanted. And like the cruel taunts and teasing, any pain was bearable to be wanted. And to be wanted by such a boy as my brother.

Monty was quick. I watched as his back convulsed and he thrust spasmodically into her. He collapsed on top of her, resting his spent body on hers. And I saw her smile. He climbed off her, his penis still swollen and swinging lazily. Blood dripped from it. I could see more blood encrusted blackly in his pubic hair. He smiled at me and began to pull on his underwear, and all I could think was what would our mother say when she saw the bloodstains on his white briefs. He winked at me and said, "Wanna give her a try?" And the throbbing returned to my head and a flush heated my skin. I looked at Denise. She lay prone and naked in front of me. She stared back at me. Beyond her, through her bedroom door, I could see her braces scattered on the floor like the remnants of a metal cocoon. She smiled at me and reached between her legs. She parted her legs even further in a vile and drunken gesture of welcome. Blood was smeared between her white thighs like a violent inkblot.

I ran. I ran as fast and as hard as I could. And behind me I could hear them laughing. The two of them, laughing at me. The sex act had changed everything. It had changed the status quo. Now they shared a secret knowledge that I was no part of. It was a reversal. A damn good one. Perhaps it was here that my love of the dramatic reversal was borne. It's as an audience member that the future playwright grows to admire the pureness of the drama. And I had been set up, sucker punched, left reeling. It should have been me and Monty laughing at her.

Our parents never found out. The effects of the gin had worn off by the time they returned late that evening, and if Monty and Denise had seemed a touch hungover the next morning, no one commented on it. Denise's puppy love for my brother escalated after that episode, only, it wasn't puppy love anymore, was it? They had shared a secret, an adult act. There had been no love involved, no sense of intimacy. It had been an act of drunken obscenity. Yet I knew that in her mind it had been intimate, it had been loving, and now she expected something more from my brother, and why wouldn't she? In her mind it was a natural progression. But in Monty's mind, nothing had changed. He continued his campaign of cruelty and, if anything, his taunts reached a new apogee in their ferociousness. He wanted nothing to do with the girl, but he couldn't shut her out completely. After all, she might tell. She might tell how the young man entrusted to watch after her safety had drunk liquor with her. How he had taken her virginity, taken her innocence.

Monty had only one sanctuary from Denise's ever-increasing need to be in his presence. The water. The lake was verboten for Denise. Her mother harbored a very vocal fear that Denise might slip and fall in the water and, unable to maneuver her metal-weighted legs, drown. Her mother was so adamant and never wavering about this fear that it had crossed over to Denise. It was second nature to her. She simply would not go near the water.

A raft anchored near the middle of the lake was Monty's refuge. When Denise's presence became overwhelming, he dove into the lake and swam out to the raft. It was made of weathered gray wood and was big enough for Monty to stretch out comfortably. As the summer wore on, most of Monty's days were spent on the raft, in isolation, where he was drenched in sun and grew ever more golden. The raft was so far out that my still-skinny body could not carry me to it. I simply lacked the strength and stamina. I sat on the shore longing for Monty's company and hating Denise, for she was the one who had driven him away from both of us. When I did see him, he smelled of his isolation. He smelled of the lake: dank, mossy, and earthen. It was a dark smell, and it did not suit him. It seemed more appropriate for me.

I don't know what he thought would happen. How it would end. We've never spoken of it, not of the ending. Did he really think Denise would tolerate losing him? She was, after all, a smart girl. She had captured him in the first place, had she not? Did he really think she would concede so easily? I knew she would not. I would not have in her position. She played her trump card. She threatened to tell. This, for Monty, was unacceptable. In our parents' eyes, Monty was unblemished. He was, after all, the immaculate child of beauty that they had created. They believed, as did we all, that he was sheer perfection, and he wanted them to go on believing just that. Anything less would not be tolerable.

This much I either witnessed firsthand or learned from Denise. The rest is sketchy. When he left our bedroom that late night, sneaking out through the window over the porch, there was no doubt in my mind that he was going to meet Denise. I could not prove this, but, as I say, there is no doubt in my mind. I assumed that she had finally coerced him into repeating their secret act. He was gone so long that my body betrayed me and I drifted off to sleep. My image of him when he returned is dreamy, sleep clouded. He shucked off his clothes and climbed into his bed. He whispered my name, but I did not respond. I sensed that that was what he wanted, for me to be asleep.

Her mother found her. It must have been the ultimate horror for her. Her greatest fear played out before her pathetic eyes. The screams awoke everybody but Monty, who had, after all, had a late night. Denise was at the water's edge, face down, unmoving. Her leg braces were embedded in the mud and silt that shored the lake. The jet-black hair that I had once longed to touch was hanging, matted and lifeless, from her skull. There were no secret rainbows in that hair. There was only death. We were drawn by her mother's screams, and I glimpsed the body before my mother covered my eyes and sent me back to the cabin. As I left, I heard my mother whisper to my father, "Thank God Monty didn't see."

Monty was in his bed, sleeping soundly, the covers pulled

over his head. At the foot of his bed, I saw his shorts and T-shirt balled up on the floor. I picked them up and unwadded them. They were still damp. I smelled them. They smelled of the lake: dank, mossy, and earthen.

And I looked down at my sleeping brother. And I knew that I would let nothing deny me the pleasure of basking in his golden light.

I loved him. Brighter than the sun burned, I loved him.

FORTY-ONE

We meet in the interview room. She is much younger than I would have suspected. Quite attractive. From her name, Anne Hunter, I somehow expected her to look, well, primitive. She places a digital voice recorder on the table between us. I stare at it. Watch the green LED blink its approval.

"So, Adam, why do you want to do an interview?"

I have not asked her to call me Adam; she has taken the liberty on her own. It is mildly annoying.

"I want to tell my side of the story, but I also want something from you."

"And what would that be?"

"Turn off the recorder."

"There's no point to an interview if I can't document what you're saying."

"Turn it off," I say. And she does. After all, I am a probable murderer telling her to do so. "I've read your coverage of my trial. It's been quite good."

"Thank you."

"You were right, by the way."

"About what? I always like to know when I'm right about something."

"About Leo Hewitt. He is involved in my case. He was there when I was arrested."

"I knew it."

"Leo Hewitt put together the case against me; he seemed to take a personal interest in it."

"That would be because he's sick of working traffic court."

"Why would the prosecutors deny his involvement with the case?"

"Because he's an embarrassment to them."

"Why?"

"Don't you know?"

"No. Tell me. Tell me everything you know about Leo Hewitt."

And she did. And after a while, she reached over and turned on her recorder and we began the interview in earnest. She asked her first question, and I knew what it would be. And I knew what my answer would be.

"Did you kill your wife?"

"No," I said. "No, I loved my wife."

FORTY-TWO

The other cubicles were deserted. The wan light from his lamp gave Leo's single cubicle a lonesome glow. He had his cigar smoldering away in the chipped ashtray, and the furniture catalog spread out in front of him, but he did not see the yards of red leather and planes of teak, the massive executive desks and expansive breakfronts. Instead, Leo saw the courtroom. In the theater of his mind, the trial played itself out before him. But the parts had been recast. For tonight's performance, the part of the assistant district attorney will be played by Leo Hewitt. And at the end of the third act, when the curtain fell, it would be Leo from whom the audience demanded a curtain call.

A uniformed cop approached Leo's cubicle. He peered

over the side, his thick eyebrows raised in amusement, and watched Leo daydream.

"Hey, Leo, you still here? Did you ever get that promotion?"

Leo, despite this unpleasant interruption, retrieved his cigar and managed a thin smile. "Not yet, Donny."

"Well, don't forget . . ."

Leo puffed the cigar back to life and played along with the old joke. "Don't worry, on my meteoric rise to the top, I'll take you with me."

"Just so you don't forget. Say, listen, you got a message from a Mister . . . Adam Lee. Says he wants to meet with ya."

Leo cocked an eyebrow at Donny. "Oh yeah?"

In the interview room, Adam sat at the bare table. A guard opened the door and let Leo in. Leo entered quietly. He took the chair across from Adam and looked at him expectantly, waiting for Adam to explain why he'd called him here. Although Leo thought he had a pretty good idea. The case was going badly for them. Still, it was damn odd that Adam would contact him and not Monty. Especially when you took into consideration that Leo officially had nothing to do with the case. But curiosity got the better of him, and here he was sitting in silence with the accused, knowing that if Bob or Paula found out, his ass would be gone for good this time. So why didn't the motherfucker speak? Some pathetic mind game to see who would blink first? Leo decided he didn't play that game and started out on the offensive.

"Look, Mr. Lee, if you're ready to cut a deal, you really oughta have your lawyer here. And besides that, we're not gonna cut you a deal. Mr. Lee, we got you."

"I read the papers, Mr. Hewitt. They kicked you off the case. To put it bluntly, you couldn't cut a deal with a chain-saw. That is, unless I were trying to beat a jaywalking ticket."

"You know, we haven't decided yet whether we're gonna push for the death penalty. Do you know what form of execution this state practices? Lethal injection. But I bet you knew that already. And for some reason, I kind of think it doesn't worry you too much. Now, if it were something unrefined— death by electrocution, say—I think that would bother you. Dying that way. Because it's not elegant. It's not refined. I think you would find it . . . pedestrian, beneath you. Of course, you're just as dead either way. And I gotta tell you, for an act of murder as cold-blooded and premeditated as yours, we're leaning more and more toward that every day." Leo wasn't sure he had used the word *pedestrian* the right way. He knew it meant someone who was walking, but he was pretty sure it meant "ordinary" or "common," too. He wanted to show Adam that he wasn't the only one who knew a couple of two-dollar words, and if he had fucked it up, Lee wasn't letting on.

"There is no *we*, Mr. Hewitt. There is only you. And re-gardless of the form it might take, the death penalty does not scare me. I'm innocent."

Leo got up to leave and said, "You called me down here for this? This is the news flash? Suspect claims he's innocent?"

Leo motioned for the guard to open the door.

"How would you describe yourself, Leo?" Leo waited for the guard, ignoring Adam. "What kind of man are you?"

"Gimme a break."

"Hungry? I think I would describe you as hungry. You put this whole case together, didn't you?"

"It was teamwork."

"You don't sound very convincing. Would you describe yourself as ambitious? Anxious to prove yourself?"

"Sure, whatever you say."

"Looking for that one case, that one opportunity to put yourself over the top. To prove yourself."

Leo motioned the guard away and turned back to Adam. "You got a point?"

"Yes, I have a point. Monty Lee is one of the most successful and highly respected trial lawyers in this state. He's connected. He plays golf with the governor. And the best he could do for his own brother at that critical moment was the errand boy at the DA's office?"

Leo scowled at this.

"My point is, why you? Why you of all people? Why would my brother call you to come see me that night?"

"Because I'm trustworthy, loyal, and kind. A faithful servant."

"Because he knew you were the office joke. The 'junior deputy assistant prosecutor.' The loser. The man who lost the biggest and most expensive trial in the state's history. The man who went from the head office to the typing pool."

"Fuck you! I may not have a fancy office like you. I may not wear Armani suits like you. My suits come off the rack and my office is a cubicle. But then again, there's not a picture of my dead wife's daddy hanging in the lobby."

"No, you don't have any of those things. The trappings of success. But that's what you're hungry for, isn't it? Success and everything that goes along with it, including respect. Maybe most importantly respect. My brother knows you're hungry. Maybe he knew you would dig a little deeper, try a little harder. Maybe he knew you'd smell a rat."

Now it was Adam who was in control. He was getting through to Leo. He could see it in Leo's eyes. It was starting to click into place. "How did you find Mrs. Herbert Watkins? Monty says it was her testimony that ruined us, more so than Violet's."

"That's because you essentially confessed to her."

"But Violet heard the same thing."

"Yes, Violet could testify to what she overheard you say to Mrs. Watkins, but to have Mrs. Watkins herself testify to what you said directly to her—that's the money shot."

"But how could you have found her?"

Leo's expression softened. The prospect of sharing his ingenuity was enticing, even if he would be sharing it with the man who was going to jail as a result of that ingenuity. "Easy. Well, it was hard, really. I didn't think I'd ever track the Watkinses down. I drove up to Linville Caverns. Nosed around. Asked questions. But who would remember a couple of tourists in a place that attracts nothing but tourists? In the end, it was just blind luck. But born out of persistence. I just happened to ask Violet whatever happened to the jacket. It was hanging in her closet, identification sewn in the lapel."

"That's exactly the kind of thing Monty knew you'd dig up. He knew you'd be persistent. Look, Leo, all I'm asking . . . all I want you to do is look up a couple of more facts."

"You're crazy. I work for the other side, remember?"

"Do you? Do you really?"

"Why should I?"

"Because you put me here."

"No, you put yourself here."

"Because I'm saying, I'm saying that maybe you missed something. Maybe you were manipulated. Maybe I was manipulated. Isn't it worth your time just to check it out? Isn't it worth your time to make sure you're not going to put away an innocent man?"

Leo looked at Adam and shook his head.

"Goddamn it! All I'm asking is that you double-check a couple of facts! If I'm guilty, then you'll just be doubly sure of it, before you—you—put someone away for life."

The two men stared at each other. Everything had been said. Now it was wholly up to Leo. Slowly, he nodded his head.

"What exactly do you want me to do?"

FORTY-THREE

Leo couldn't get over how pretty she was. He had interviewed her several months ago, but he'd forgotten Rosalyn Wahlberg was such a knockout.

"I'm sorry, but Mr. Lee is out of town on business this whole month."

"He's in jail. I know. I'm Leo Hewitt. I interviewed you briefly in October."

"I remember you. I thought I was finished with all of that."

"You are. Adam sent me. He needs your help."

"But don't you work for the other side?"

"It's a long story."

She used her key to open Adam's office door. Once inside, Rosalyn switched on the desk lamp and pulled the dust cover off the computer keyboard.

"What do you know about computers?"

"I don't bother them, they don't bother me."

"Well, come here. I'll give you your first lesson."

Leo looked suspiciously at the machine, then at Rosalyn.

"Sit down. Okay, now turn it on. Right back there. That's it. There. See, you're a natural." Leo smiled gratefully at her. "Okay, hit enter. The big one, to the right. Uh-oh, I don't have the password."

Leo fumbled through his pockets and pulled out a slip of paper. "I've got it." He typed in the password, and a list of functions popped up on the screen. Rosalyn leaned over Leo's shoulder. Her smell was earthy and sweet.

"How long have you worked for Adam?"

"Oh, God, it's been years and years now. I started as a temp. His secretary quit on him after her car was vandalized in the parking garage. I guess it spooked her."

"And he's seemed to be a pretty straight guy all this time?"

"Up until now, yes." The computer belched out a short electronic warble to indicate that it was ready to go.

"Well, tell it what you want it to do," Rosalyn said. Leo selected the search function. Another menu appeared on the screen. It read:

SEARCH: _ BY FINANCIAL INSTITUTION
_ BY ACCOUNT NUMBER

_ **BY NAME**
_ **BY TRANSACTION**

Leo selected *BY NAME.* "I think I'm getting the hang of this." The screen read: *ENTER NAME.* Leo typed in his own name and social security number. After about ten seconds every financial account Leo had ever opened was listed on the screen. From his first savings account as a teenager to various CDs and IRAs opened and long since cashed out. He clicked on his current checking account and saw the dutiful deposits of his paycheck along with various withdrawals.

"This can't be legal."

"I would tend to doubt that myself."

"How is it even possible?"

"This is Lawson Systems Financial Risk Management. We sell peace of mind to other, larger firms who don't want to take on the liability of doing it in-house. Adam's job is to find people's assets. Sometimes to find out if they're hiding those assets. And if so, where. You think when real money is on the line they just pull your credit report? No, they let someone like Adam look at everything. No, I doubt it's legal, but it happens every day."

Leo entered *CONSTANCE PERKINS* and fed in her Social Security number. A bank statement filled the screen. Leo could feel Rosalyn brushing up against him to point to a key. "Use this key to page through it."

Leo paged through Violet's bank records, scanning each

transaction. Mostly, there were deposits and withdrawals of a few hundred dollars each. Then he saw a deposit of twenty thousand dollars on the thirty-first of October.

"I'll be damned."

"Is that what you were looking for?"

"Oh yeah. Is there any way to find out what account the twenty thousand came out of?"

"Adam could probably do it, but I wouldn't know where to begin. Maybe if we knew where to start looking. If you had an account number or a name."

Leo typed in *MONTGOMERY LEE.*

"Monty?"

"Yeah, you ever met him?"

"I went out with him once."

"You dated him?"

"Once. We went out once."

Monty's financial history—loans, mortgage, credit report, investments—popped onto the screen. He had three separate bank accounts. Over the course of three months, there were more cash withdrawals, on average, than there were, say, the three months prior to that. Nothing big, nothing that stood out. Seven hundred dollars here, twelve hundred there—pocket money for a man-about-town like Monty Lee. Only problem was, these excess cash withdrawals added up to roughly twenty thousand dollars more cash than Monty had ever used in any other three-month period. Maybe he was a recovering gambler; maybe he had had a relapse, gone on a three-month gambling binge at the dog tracks. Maybe he had developed a taste for designer drugs, then given them up. It didn't really matter, though, did it? They were relatively small withdrawals—unusual, perhaps, in the long run, but easily explainable in any number of ways.

"Why only once?"

"He seemed more interested in Adam than me."

"How do you mean?"

"Well, he would ask me things. Like had Adam ever come on to me."

"And what did you tell him?"

"The truth. That Adam would never do something like that. At least that's what I used to think before all of this. Anyway, Monty never called me again after that one night. And I was glad. I mean, he may be the city's most eligible bachelor, but he just seemed like a creep to me."

Leo watched financial statements shuffle across the computer screen. He considered what Rosalyn had said about Monty Lee. He decided she was a smart girl.

"So, are you dating anybody now?"

FORTY-FOUR

Violet answered the door dressed only in a ratty bathrobe. "Mr. Hewitt. Is everything okay?" She opened the door wider to let Leo inside. The five aluminum steps that led up to the trailer groaned in protest under Leo's weight. For a moment, he seriously wondered if the steps would simply collapse. He could see places at the joints where rust had completely eaten through them. But they held, and he gratefully entered Violet's squalid trailer.

Packing boxes were set out on every available surface. Some were sealed shut; others overflowed with clothing and dirty kitchen wares.

"You'll have to excuse the mess. I'm moving next week." She retrieved a beer bottle stuck between two couch cushions and took a long swig from it. With her head upturned, the

229

bathrobe fell open, revealing the swell of her breasts and the beginnings of her pubic hair. She made no effort to cover herself.

"Moving up in the world, Violet?"

"Sure, why not?"

"With a little help from Monty?"

Violet closed the robe, belting it tightly. "Monty? Who's that?"

"C'mon, Violet. I've had a really hard week."

"Oh! Monty! He's that guy from *Let's Make a Deal*, right?"

"Yeah. Yeah, he is. And you made a deal with him, didn't you, Violet? About twenty thousand deals."

FORTY-FIVE

Paula fine-tuned her makeup in the mirror that hung on the back of her office door. Leo opened the door without knocking, and Paula frowned as her reflection slid away from her.

"Leo. Come on in, it's good to see you," she said with as much sarcasm as she could muster, which wasn't much. It would be bad karma, not to mention hell on the frown lines. She wanted to stay in good spirits today. She was due in court in twenty minutes, and every bit of equilibrium she could hold on to would be an asset.

"We need to talk," Leo said.

Paula closed the office door and resumed studying her reflection. She outlined her thin lips with a tube of pale lipstick. "Court's in twenty minutes. Today's the big day. Adam

Lee is gonna testify. You gonna be there to give me moral support?"

"Not today. I gotta talk to you about something."

Paula struggled with a pair of opal earrings, small enough to be overlooked, but there nonetheless to accent her femininity.

"Adam Lee might be innocent."

"Uh-huh, uh-huh, yeah, great."

"I'm serious. I've uncovered evidence that tends to indicate Mr. Lee's—"

"Stop." Paula got the last earring in and turned on Leo. "I don't care. It doesn't matter. It's a little late in the game for that sort of thing, don't you think? Isn't this dangerously close to the kind of thinking that messed up your life in the first place?"

"But I found out that—"

"I don't care if you just found out he's Jesus Christ come down from the cross. Because I'm nailing his ass back up there. I'm gonna crucify the fucker again." She checked herself in the mirror and saw Leo's bowed head behind her. "That's my job, Leo. That's what I do. It's what you used to do. I have no choice."

"He may be innocent."

"So?"

"So how can you prosecute an innocent man?"

"You can't be serious with this. I don't know that he's innocent. And neither do you. That's for the jury to decide."

"That's what I'm trying to tell you, if you'd just listen to me."

"Look, Leo, wise up, okay? You're a good lawyer, but you can't hang with the men. You're pathetic. Now why don't you be a good little robot and go back to your cubicle."

She checked her look one last time and gathered her papers for court.

"And get used to that cubicle, Leo. You'll be working there for a very, very long time."

FORTY-SIX

Today the courtroom is packed with spectators. An artist scribbles furiously to capture my face. I remain expressionless, but I know that the artist will sketch in faint lines around my mouth to connote sadness or guilt. We watch as the jury files in. None of them look at me. They never do. Monty sits beside me at the defense table. He leans and whispers into my ear, "Today I am my brother's keeper." His breath is warm, humid, and pleasant so close to me. Even now, I take comfort and delight in his closeness. He is golden.

Have I mentioned that I love him? I do, oh, I do.

Monty stands and addresses Judge Cray. "Your Honor, the defense would like to call as its last witness the defendant, Mr. Adam Lee."

As the bailiff swears me in, my hand trembles. I concentrate to make it stop, lest one of the jurors interpret it as a sign of guilt and make a premature decision. Once I am seated, Monty stands before me. He gives me a wan smile and a slight nod of his head. This, of course, is for the benefit of the jury.

"Mr. Lee, after everything that's gone on before this moment, there's really only one question that matters. I'll ask it point-blank. Adam Lee, did you murder your wife?"

"No," I say, "No, I loved my wife."

FORTY-SEVEN

The office cubicles were busy now. Like insects building a colony, the office workers busied themselves with their daily rituals. The sounds of printers humming, copy machines laboring, and the quiet murmur of conversations surrounded Leo. He heard none of it. The sounds of Paula's last words to him reverberated in his head. The downward sneer of her sterile mouth. The hard glint in her unforgiving eyes. And her words echoed. He stared into space, seeing only her, and in his hands he held a pencil. He bent the pencil slightly with his fists. The pressure on the pencil was building slowly and the wood was beginning to crack minutely; small yellow splinters danced to the surface at the pressure mark. It had reached its breaking point. The pencil snapped. So did Leo.

A rage consumed him. A rage that could not be held in.

A sound escaped his throat, and a secretary passing by on her way to the water cooler stopped and stared at him. Her expression was akin to that of a little girl who has just found a razor blade in her Halloween apple. Leo stared at her and growled. She ducked her head and hurried away. Leo sprang to his feet and looked around wildly, looked for some way to vent this anger before it swallowed him whole. He stared down at his desk, the laminate peeling away from the cheap mass-produced surface, and it seemed to suddenly symbolize everything that had ever gone wrong in his life. Another growl escaped his throat and he overturned the desk. He did not simply push it over, but flipped it, sent it spinning into the air. As it crashed down, the cheap pressboard splintered and cracked apart. Not satisfied, Leo kicked out at the walls of his cubicle, and the cheap material buckled. The office grew dead quiet except for the sounds of Leo's rage. The workers interrupted their tasks and stared at him. One young man cowered under his desk, sure that Leo would soon pull out an automatic weapon and begin gunning people down.

"What are ya? Buncha good little robots?" he shouted at them. He shook the cubicle walls violently, sending them heaving back and forth. The metal strips that held the cubicle walls together began to twist and come apart. The walls began to wobble and shake and then started to tumble down, and soon, like dominoes, all the cubicles fell over and came apart.

FORTY-EIGHT

"So, you were only joking?"

"Yes. I never dreamed . . ."

"Would you describe yourself as a good husband?"

"As good a husband as I could be. I tried to be, I really did try to be a good husband."

"And how would you describe your affair with Constance Perkins in the context of being a good husband?"

"As a mistake. I knew it was wrong. That's what the weekend was for. To put an end to it. To break it off."

"How did Ms. Perkins react when you told her the relationship was over?"

"She was angry. Very angry. I guess she still is."

From my position on the witness stand, I am the first to see Leo when he opens the door to the courtroom. I have to suppress a mischievous grin when I see him. His chest is comically puffed out in a parody of righteous pride. He makes his way down the aisle, but he doesn't stop to take a seat. Spectators crane their heads to see him. It is quite dramatic, almost overly so, but, I must confess, I had at that time grown most fond of high drama.

He approaches the bench, still beaming with righteousness. "Your Honor, I have new evidence that directly relates to this trial. It will affect the outcome of this trial. I respectfully ask the court's permission to confer with Adam Lee."

The courtroom is silent. I know this will be Leo's finest hour. The entire court stares at him. The judge's expression is almost comical. "Are you kidding?" he asks. I try my best to look as amazed as the others. I hope the sketch artist can adequately capture my astonishment. If this isn't front-page material, then nothing is.

Leo stands boldly before the judge and takes a deep breath, and for one horrifying moment I am certain that he will lose his nerve, whimper mildly, and slink away. But I have not underestimated Mr. Hewitt; he performs admirably. "No, sir," he says to the judge. "I am not kidding. I am in possession of evidence that could directly affect the outcome of this trial."

Monty, as if on cue, rushes forward. He too plays his part with aplomb. "Your Honor, we have no wish to speak with this . . . individual. We respectfully ask that you have him removed from the courtroom."

Ms. Manning grins stupidly and nods her head in silent

agreement. If it were in my power to give the judge a gavel that he could use to shake at Leo as he spoke, I would, but some things are beyond my control. The judge's voice, however, carries more dramatic weight than any prop ever could. "Sir, you may leave this courtroom voluntarily, or—"

And now for the reversal. Everything shifts. What you think will happen does not; in fact, just the opposite occurs. The one thing no one in the audience expects to happen, happens. I speak. And I say the one thing no one expects me to say. "No," I say, and all heads turn toward me. "I want to talk with him."

"Absolutely not!" Monty bellows. I smile at him.

"Bailiff, please escort the jury out of the courtroom until we can get this mess settled." The bailiff does so, and Leo crosses the stage to confer with me. We hold our heads together and he whispers dark secrets to me, secrets I already know. We both turn our heads when Ms. Manning speaks to the judge.

"Your Honor, this is highly unusual."

"If I'm not mistaken, Ms. Manning, he's a member of *your* team. Correct?" Ms. Manning doesn't respond. The judge looks past her to the district attorney. "He does work for your office, doesn't he, Mr. Fox?"

Fox begins to respond, but I interrupt him, concerned that he may ad-lib, insert a line that isn't in the script. "Your Honor," I say, "based on information I've just received, I would like to dismiss my attorney."

Monty is in shock, as well he should be. "Adam, are you crazy?"

The judge sighs and hangs his head. "I'm inclined to agree with your brother, Mr. Lee. This is crazy. This isn't a Perry Mason novel. I'm not the cantankerous old judge with a heart of gold. In fact, I'm starting to get angry."

Ms. Manning is having none of it. "He's about to be found guilty of murder; of course he wants to change counsel."

"Do I have the right to dismiss my attorney or not?" I ask. The judge sighs, and I know that suddenly he has allowed me to recast him. He is the cantankerous old judge with a heart of gold.

"Oh, you have the right all right, but let me tell you right now, we're not stopping this trial. Ms. Manning is correct. This looks an awful lot like the actions of a desperate man."

"Fine. The trial goes on. I dismiss my attorney, Montgomery Lee."

"Adam!"

"And name as my new attorney Leo Hewitt."

"Adam, what in the name of God are you doing? This is insanity!"

I ignore Monty and study Leo instead. He backs away from me and shakes his head. He is scared. He hadn't bargained on me calling him to task, but I have faith in my loyal and trusty servant.

We all wait for his assent or dissent, but he offers neither. He merely stares at me and imperceptibly shakes his head.

The judge asks, "Well, Mr. Hewitt? Are you Adam Lee's attorney or not?"

"He can't," the Manning woman says, her carefully applied makeup not coming close to disguising the purple bloom of anger in her flesh. She says each word with deliberate, barely controlled fury. "He works for the district attorney's office."

Still no word from Leo. We all wait. But, as I said, I have faith.

"Well?" the judge asks.

Leo breaks his silence and says, "No."

Ms. Manning smiles wickedly. The flush retreats from her face, leaving scarlet trails down her neck. She believes she has won. She believes in Leo's weakness. For one uneasy moment, I too believe she has won, but, like her, I also believe in Leo's weakness, and know that all is not lost.

Leo turns to look directly in Ms. Manning's eyes. "No. I don't work for the district attorney's office. I quit." He turns now to the judge. "And to answer your question, Judge Cray, yes, I am Adam Lee's attorney, and, in light of new evidence, I would like to dismiss Adam Lee as the defense's final witness and call instead Mr. Montgomery Lee to the stand."

FORTY-NINE

It felt good. It felt damn good. Leo knew he was on like never before. He was cooking with gas. Now if he could just get Monty to squirm a little. The two-day interruption in the trial had been tough. He could have still backed out, let Adam find another lawyer. He wanted to do just that, because for some reason, the urge to just back out was overwhelming. He found that he was scared. But scared of what? Of succeeding? Of doing the one thing he had dreamed of doing? Well, yes, actually, he was. But in the end, he knew that after the grandstand he'd pulled in court two days before, there was no point in not seeing it through to the end. He had it all. All the proof, all the evidence, why not take all the glory? Why not crush Bob Fox and Paula Manning under his heel in the process? Why not make them look like boobs? Why not do to them what they had done to him? Why not?

The only obstacle would be Monty Lee himself. Leo had evidence, but he also knew that evidence was never enough. Not in a jury trial. He had to make the jury believe, not just show them the facts, but actually make them believe that Montgomery Lee was a monster. And so far it wasn't working. Leo was doing everything right. It was all coming together— except for Monty's smug charm. Half the women on the jury were creaming their undies over him, and the men were probably doing the same. Monty was just that impressive. He answered the questions without hesitation. He looked not at all nervous. And he responded to Leo as though Leo were a fly, a pest, a nuisance, but certainly not a danger. And that demeanor was getting across to the jury. He had to make Monty squirm.

"Now, what I don't understand, Mr. Lee, is what would have been Adam Lee's motive for this murder?"

"Objection. Calls for speculation."

Leo gave Paula a grateful smile. If Monty wasn't going to show any discomfort, at least he could count on Paula to look hot and bothered. "As the defendant's ex–defense attorney, he's infinitely qualified to speculate on assumed motive."

"Overruled. Let's keep moving."

Leo waited for Paula to sit back down. He noticed that her makeup seemed a bit overdone today, a little too thick. One of her earrings was crooked. There was a small run in one leg of her stockings. Had Judge Elizabeth Duran been here, she might have thought Paula looked, in fact, a little bit like a hooker in search of a twenty-dollar blowjob.

"Answer the question, please. What would have been your brother's motive for murder?"

"Because Adam stood to profit from his wife's death. Well over forty million dollars."

"Did you prepare Ms. Lee's will?"

"Yes."

"And she left her entire estate to her husband, Adam Lee?"

"No. She left it all to her son, Albert Lee."

"I don't understand. That sounds to me like Albert Lee would be the only person who could profit from the murder."

"No. Since Albert is not legally competent, Adam, as his legal guardian, would have complete control over all of Albert's assets. Albert's inheritance would, in essence, become Adam's property."

Monty looked past Leo to his brother sitting alone at the defense table. He gave Adam a slight shrug of the shoulder and an imperceptibly raised eyebrow. The gestures seemed to say, *Sorry, but it's your own fault, don't blame me.* None of this, of course, was lost on the jury. Or Leo. *Send all the signals you want,* Leo thought. *You smug bastard, you don't even see it coming, do you? These questions are nothing to you. Why aren't you worried, just a little? How can you stay so calm?* Then it hit him. Was it possible? Had he overestimated the man? Was that why he was so complacent? Could it be that he really didn't see it coming?

"And if Adam Lee is found guilty of this crime, what happens to the money?"

"It would still go to his son, Albert."

"So, Adam Lee would get the money even if he was found guilty?"

"No. You don't get it. You can't profit from a crime. The inheritance would still be Albert's, but Adam couldn't touch it."

"But Albert's legal guardian could?"

"Yes."

"And who would become Albert's legal guardian if Adam Lee were convicted of this crime?"

Paula objected. "Your Honor, this is going nowhere. All of this ground has been covered before."

Well, Leo thought, as always, he could still get a rise from Paula. Monty Lee, however, looked like he was waiting for a limousine to the inaugural ball. "Judge, I assure you this is most definitely going somewhere."

"Overruled. Get to your point, Mr. Hewitt."

"Who would become Albert's legal guardian if Adam Lee were to be convicted of this crime?"

"I'm not sure what provisions Adam and Rachel made for such an eventuality."

"So you don't know who would become Albert's legal guardian?"

"I believe that's what I just said."

Getting a little testy there, aren't you, my friend? Monty, old pal.

Is the limo starting to look a little late for the ball? Leo grabbed a sheaf of papers from the defense table. He handed a copy to Paula and one to the judge. "Your Honor, I'd like to enter this into evidence," Leo said and handed a copy to Monty. "Mr. Lee, could you take a look at this document and tell me if you recognize it?"

Monty thumbed through the pages and stopped suddenly. Leo thought he could detect a slight tremor run through Monty's hands. An imperceptible tremor, as imperceptible as his smug shrug of the shoulders earlier. *Something wrong, Monty? Maybe the limousine driver got lost. Don't worry, I'm sure they'll delay the inauguration until you arrive.*

"Mr. Lee, do you recognize this document?"

"I'm not sure." His voice was thick. It rattled with phlegm, trembled with . . . could it be? Yes, it was fear. Leo had heard it clearly. Fear. He was sure the jury had heard it, too. Hell, Helen Keller could have heard it.

Leo leaned over Monty and thumbed through the document to the last page. "Is this your signature?"

Monty didn't answer. *What's the matter, Monty? Cat got your tongue? Or maybe the limo ran it over.*

"Mr. Lee, is this your signature?"

"It appears to be."

"Could you tell the court what type of document this is?"

"It's a custody agreement."

"And whose custody does it concern?"

Monty didn't answer. Leo noticed how Monty stared at

the paper. He stared at it as though it were a poisonous snake someone had just dropped in his lap, and any movement, any sound might provoke it to strike.

"Isn't it true, Mr. Lee, that this document names you as the legal guardian of Albert Lee should his natural parents be unable to function as his legal guardians?"

Monty could only remain motionless, soundless. He looked as though he believed the snake would just slither away if he pretended to be asleep.

"Isn't it true, Mr. Lee, that if your brother, Adam Lee, is found guilty of murder, you stand to gain control of more than forty million dollars?"

The snake had struck, the bite deep and solid. He could stop pretending now. Now it didn't matter, the poison had been unleashed.

"I wish to invoke my Fifth Amendment privileges."

A smile crossed Leo's lips. Imperceptible, he hoped. He had won. From the corner of his eye, he could see one of the jurors shake her head in disgust, disgust with Monty's cowardice. The Fifth Amendment was for cowards. For cowards and the guilty.

"I understand. In that case, let's talk about something different. Let's talk about Violet Perkins."

FIFTY

LEE ACQUITTED, BROTHER CHARGED

by Anne Hunter
staff writer

Last month's bizarre twist in the already bizarre Lee trial is likely to result in the conviction of Montgomery Lee for the murder of Rachel Lee, prosecutors say. Near the end of Adam Lee's trial for the murder of his wife, Rachel, Mr. Lee dismissed his brother, Montgomery, as his attorney and named former junior deputy prosecutor Leo Hewitt as his new counsel. New evidence brought forth by Mr. Hewitt indicated to the court that Montgomery Lee was a more likely suspect. Adam Lee was found not guilty of the crime, and today Montgomery Lee was formally charged with the murder of his brother's wife. In an exclusive interview with the *Tribune* from jail a month ago, Adam Lee stated that he did not know who killed his wife, but had "suspicions." Mr. Lee also said—

The thought. The thought interrupted his reading. It was interrupting everything lately. Leo folded the paper and put the thought away. He reached for his cigar. It was smoldering away elegantly in a cut lead crystal ashtray. He grabbed it and puffed it back to life. And the thought came back. That was the trouble with pesky thoughts; you could put them away, but they just kept coming back. And here it was again. It kept popping into his mind unbidden. He shoved the thought to a vacant corner of his mind and left it there. *Stay away, bad thought, you're not welcome around here anymore.* He was going to concentrate on being happy. And why wasn't he as happy as he felt he ought to be? He knew he should be happy (there, the thought was gone), and for the most part he was. Hell— fuck, for the most part—he *was* happy. His dreams, despite the fact that he had begun to believe that they never would, were beginning to come true. The clothes, the office, the money, the prestige. The respect. He had won all of that by winning Adam Lee his freedom. And as an added bonus, he had been out four times with Rosalyn Wahlberg, and, judging from how heated things had gotten during that fourth date, number five would be his lucky number. He looked at his watch—five minutes before Adam was due to show up. A good-bye kiss before he left for Madagascar. An extended vacation, Adam had called it. But Leo couldn't help but be struck by the fact that Madagascar was one of a handful of countries with no extradition agreement with the United States. Funny, wasn't it? Of course, if something—some small fact, say—should turn up, he couldn't be tried for the same crime twice anyway. But why take chances? Just look what our wonderful legal system had already put the man through. Once bitten, twice shy, right? You never knew what might happen; someone might want to charge him with a new crime altogether. Best to be safe. Leo didn't blame the guy one bit. You just never knew what was gonna happen. Just look at the case against Monty Lee. Why, just last week it had seemed airtight, but now things were starting to look different. Leo had heard rumblings from the DA's office (not that he was welcome there, by any means, but people loved to talk, especially if there was dirt involved), rumblings that the case against Monty Lee wasn't as rosy as their statements to the press would lead one to believe. Certain inconsistencies were turning up. Little things like his ironclad alibi. It was impenetrable. They were trying to punch a few holes in it, and who knew, maybe they would, but Leo doubted it. Little things like the signatures on that custody agreement. It seemed that they might be the least bit forged. The handwriting analysts seemed to think so anyway. Sometimes, little things meant a lot. The DA's office said that these were obstacles that they would easily resolve, but Leo doubted it. Now why on earth would he doubt that? After all, he had practically indicted the man himself, so why would he have doubts? And, oh, here he was, back at the unpleasant thought. He gave in to the thought, saw no point in fighting it any longer. He took the thought out, twirled it around a bit, examined it. It was an image really. Yes, more of an image than an actual thought. An image that would almost certainly lead to a whole slew of unpleasant thoughts, and unpleasant thoughts wouldn't go well with the new mahogany desk and crystal ashtray, would they? It was an image of eyes, was what it was. An image of Monty Lee's eyes. The eyes don't lie. No, the eyes don't lie. And Monty Lee never saw it coming. He never saw it coming. Right up till the end, he never saw it. If he had done the things Leo had accused him of doing, then how could he have not seen it coming? The surprise, the astonishment. The eyes don't lie. Monty Lee was either the cockiest, most self-assured liar the world had ever known, or he—

(No, best not to think about that. Put the thought away.)

(Just put it away!)

Or he was—

(No! Put the thought away. Now!)

Or he was innocent.

Leo looked up when he heard Adam clearing his throat. "Sorry. Daydreaming, I guess."

"Why dream? Haven't your dreams come true?"

"More or less."

"More, it looks to me. Your office is quite handsome. I'm sure that you will prosper here. I imagine you've generated many clients already and several retainers as well, I'm sure. How many?"

"Fifteen."

"Fifteen. Yes, you will prosper. And so will I. In any case, I'm on my way to the airport. I just wanted to stop by and thank you one last time."

"You have nothing to thank me for."

"No, I have everything to thank you for."

"Well, it was a hell of a case, I'll say that much."

"Yes, but it turned out quite all right, for both of us."

"Not for Monty, though."

"No, not for Monty."

Leo puffed on his cigar, and the two men stood in silence.

Adam spoke first. "In any case, I just wanted to say thank you." He turned to leave.

"Wait a minute."

"Yes?"

"I just—"

"Yes?"

"You killed her, didn't you?"

Adam didn't hesitate. "Of course I killed her. I thought you knew. Why, you almost seem surprised."

"Why?"

"Why what?"

"Why . . . Why did you kill her?"

"You mean you don't know? Of course you know. I killed her because I loved her. Because she loved me."

"Do you kill everyone you love?"

"More or less, sometimes more. Look, Leo, why be coy? You know it all already."

"I do?"

"Absolutely. Everything you dug up for that woman attorney to steal away from you was absolutely true. All of it. You had it all right from the beginning."

"You tricked me."

"Tricked you? Please. You can't be that blind. You may have tricked yourself, fooled yourself into believing what you wanted to believe. She stole the glory from you, Leo. And you stole it back. It's as simple as that. You are not going to stand there with that sniveling look on your face and expect me to believe you were chasing your ideals? You were chasing a dollar bill on a string."

"But why set up your brother, why make him pay for your crimes?"

"Somebody had to pay. Why not Monty? It's beyond your scope of knowledge, but believe me, Monty owed a debt."

"But you set him up from the beginning. You planned it from the start."

"He was insurance, nothing more. The ruses I constructed are made of paper. They will degrade quickly. Even a third-rate lawyer could win him his freedom. I established bank accounts in his name, slowly extracted the money, then deposited the cash funds into an account for Violet. I sent her the bank statement along with an anonymous note indicating that twenty thousand dollars could purchase a trailer almost anywhere. And the guardianship, nothing more than a cheap forgery. I ultimately convinced Rachel to sign, but Monty—ever the wise one—refused. So I signed his name myself. Of course it will never hold up to close scrutiny, but, then again, I don't need it to. In fact, I never seriously thought I would ever be forced to use it at all. I never expected the blame to go past Albert. Yes, that is repulsive, I know, but when you really consider it, I never hurt Albert. I'm sure none of this ever penetrated his dark world. But, as I say, I never expected it to go past him. I never expected more than a small tragedy that wouldn't make it to page five in the local paper. I never expected you. No. But I planned for you. The bank accounts, the guardianship, all in reserve for future use. And, as I say, Monty is not blameless. He owed; trust me, he owed."

Leo's world was a little grayer than it had been five minutes ago. He knew it was true. Every word of it. Even the bit about the dollar bill on a string. But parts of it seemed to still be missing, unnecessary chances taken. There were certain . . . inconsistencies, if you will.

"Why wait so long? Why let things get so out of control before you used your plan? You damned well almost went to prison. How could you know that I would take your bait?"

"Anyone would have taken it. That was what it was there for. I could have called any investigator at any time. But the irony of using you to do my bidding was overwhelmingly intoxicating. I just couldn't resist. Why wait till things seemed their darkest before making my move? The drama was a factor, but I also wanted to be acquitted. Double jeopardy and all that."

The drama? Leo wasn't sure he'd heard him correctly. Did the guy really say that the drama was a factor? A spasm, like the chill after a swallow of strong liquor, shot through Leo's intestines. It was a spasm of fear. He guessed that maybe it could be true that he'd known on some level that the guy was a murderer, but this he'd never dreamed of. Insanity scared him. Drama? It sounded maybe not insane exactly, but certainly it was the language of the disturbed. Like "the drama" was a motivating factor in most people's everyday decisions. *Why'd you spank your dog, Frank? Well, you know, he peed on the carpet and, plus, you know, the drama was a factor.*

"Huh," Leo said dumbly, from far away.

"Double jeopardy. You are familiar—"

"Can't be tried for the same crime twice."

"See, you are a good lawyer. Nothing third-rate about you."

"But you can be tried for other crimes. Forgery, perjury, conspiracy, illegal transfer of funds, and plenty more. I'm sure it would add up to thirty years or more."

"And who would bring the charges? You? I doubt it. You would be acknowledging that I was the second killer you've set free. But don't beat yourself up over it. You can still sleep well at night. I was simply a pathetic man leading a life of quiet desperation."

Absurdly, Leo found himself thinking of Samuel Abdul, the man who had scammed his mother out of his dead father's insurance money. He remembered the prosecutor who put Abdul away and how he had inspired Leo to become a prosecutor too. To help people like his mother. And now it had come to this? Was this what he was about now? Was this what he had aspired to be? Christ. Could time really change a person like that?

"You needn't worry. I won't kill again."

"I'll make sure of it." It was an empty threat, and they both knew it.

"Will you? Will you really? And when the news gets out of what you've done, yes, what you have done, what will happen to your beautiful new office, your fifteen retainers, your Armani jacket. Your newfound respect. Would you really be willing to sacrifice all of this? Muddy your name yet again? And for what? Me?"

Leo stared at Adam, his eyes burning with hatred. It was the hatred that can only come from being bested. Insane or not, the man had bested him.

He lowered his eyes.

"I guess there was another reason I picked you."

And Leo lifted his eyes in time to see the office door close as Adam Lee walked out of his life forever.

FIFTY-ONE

When I think of the taking of a human life, I find that it bothers me only slightly. But, truth be told, I seldom think of it. Why should I? What is done—is done. I can take it back no more than the sun can take back its light. Yes, of course, I admit that I sometimes think of these things. Sometimes I think of Rachel's dead eyes staring, accusatory, and the flies buzzing lazily around her inert form, feeding and laying eggs in pools of her coagulating blood. I think of the sound of her skull collapsing under the solid weight of lead crystal when I struck her from behind. The sound of it, wet and hard, and, I think, somehow pressurized as though the bad thoughts were finally escaping her head.

I think of Albert. I see him there in the living room as I close the door on him to leave him sealed in with the corpse of his mother, my wife, for two days. I wonder if he ever even realized that she was dead. If he did, I imagine those nights were long and dark for him. I think of Albert in his dark place, and I feel no remorse. Why should I? I did not put him there.

I think of Monty and the golden light that I stole from him, and I feel no remorse. Perhaps I should, but I do not. I feel instead a sense of pride, a sense of cunning. I feel a sense of completeness in the knowledge that life has, at long last, come full circle. Now I am the golden one. Now he is in the dark place. All debts are paid. It is as it should be.

But, as I say, I seldom think of these things. Why should I? I am a new man now. A new man with a new home. I like this new home. It is foreign and therefore familiar. The days are long and hot and sun choked. The nights are cool and pass quickly. It suits me, I think. I also find that I no longer have a taste for drama. It bores me. Or, rather, boredom excites me.

I spend a great deal of my time at the beach. In my old life, I had never seen the ocean. It is the perfect pairing of dark and light. On the beach, in the hot salty sand, the light is inescapable. There is no way to avoid it. It will suffocate you if you let it. And should you feel the sun overwhelming you, the rays forcing themselves into your mouth and down your throat, there is one convenient cure. The ocean itself. It grows darker and more oppressive the farther out you venture, so you can gauge your own needs, take only the correct dose. I once went too far out and felt the thousands of feet of dark water yawning under me, wanting to swallow me and take me down forever. Phantom fingers of cool water would reach out from the warm depths, swirl around my legs, caressing me as a demonic lover might, seducing me to come with her to her unnamed depths. Forever. I resisted.

I have met someone new. A new partner for the new man. It seemed appropriate. I, too, have desires, passions. I met her at the beach. She came up to me golden and wet, sleek and delicious. Her name is Gail. I should have known from her name. I should have known from the tingling excitement I felt in her presence. From the attraction that coursed between us—we attract what we need. We needed each other. Yes, I believe that now. I needed her. As the mouse needs the comforting, squeezing death of the snake, as the deer needs the hunter's bullet, as the fly needs to feel the sticky grasp of the spider's web, I needed her. And she me.

I tell her that I want to go for a walk on the beach, alone, to clear my head and settle my thoughts. She nods in agreement and offers me a loving smile. She understands, I think. She understands me and is content to let me be my own entity, to let me exist apart from her and yet be with her. When I return, her eyes are red rimmed and swollen; tear tracks are drying into desert paths in her heavy makeup. She tells me that she can't help it, that she loves me so much that she just goes crazy from it. I go to her and comfort her. I tell her that everything is fine. That we are fine. Soon her smile returns and she leads me to the bedroom. This is a scene that will be repeated many times.

She tells me that I don't love her, that I never have and never will. She says that she loves me and I hate her. That I think she's crazy. That I hate her and am afraid of her. I tell her that I am not afraid, that I do not think she is crazy. *Liar*, she screams, and picks at the scabs in her scalp. *Liar*, she screams, and pulls out clumps of her hair. *Liar*, she screams, and rips open her flesh. *Why do you hate me so? You do hate me. Admit it.*

No, I say. *No. I love you.*